Milou in May

Louis Malle began his career as a film director in 1957 with
L'Ascenseur pour l'échaufaud. Since then his work has alternated
between feature films and documentaries and includes such
notable films as *Zazie dans le Métro*, *Le Voleur*, *Phantom India*,
Atlantic City, *My Dinner with André*, and his two meditations on
France during the Second World War: *Lacombe, Lucien* and *Au
revoir les enfants*.

Jean-Claude Carrière has had a distinguished career as a writer.
He wrote six screenplays with Luis Buñuel including *The
Discreet Charm of the Bourgeoisie*. He has also worked with Peter
Brook on *The Mahabharata* as well as with Milos Forman on
Valmont and Philip Kaufman on *The Unbearable Lightness of
Being*.

Also by Louis Malle

AU REVOIR LES ENFANTS
and
LACOMBE, LUCIEN

Milou in May

LOUIS MALLE *and*
JEAN-CLAUDE CARRIÈRE

Translated by
Jayne Pilling

faber and faber
LONDON · BOSTON

First published in 1990
by Faber and Faber Limited
3 Queen Square London WCIN 3AU

Photoset by Wilmaset, Birkenhead, Wirral
Printed in Great Britain
by Richard Clay Ltd, Bungay, Suffolk

A CIP record for this book
is available from the British Library
ISBN 0–571–14497–7

Contents

Louis Malle on location.

Memories are always vague, and when they are not they are
usually wrong because we unconsciously distort them to make
them sharp and clear. Take 1968, a year which turned America
and Europe upside-down, and which today each of us
remembers differently. That May – when the barricades were
going up in the Latin Quarter in Paris – a friend of ours
happened to be cruising round the Mediterranean on a
luxurious boat, with absolutely nothing to do but listen to the
radio from dawn to dusk. The sound of the tear-gas grenades
was so amplified and so appalling that it made them seem like
enormous shells. Paris, she thought, was bleeding, was burning,
and the cruise was ruined.

But for other people – for Louis and myself, for example,
who happened to be together in Paris, though we were too old
to be part of the student world – the memories are different,
almost the opposite. Louis, who had just come back from a long
journey through India with a series of very beautiful films and a
remarkable beard, observed these first few days with great
astonishment; so did I, though at the time I had a Czech film-
maker named Milos Forman staying with me who endlessly
repeated in depressed tones: 'But why on earth are you so intent
on raising the red flag when we are having so much trouble
pulling it down?'

And then a party mood took over, a real celebration, a
conversation without end. We were obsessed with the notion
that the world could be remade – and remade immediately. We
were drunk with spring. And that's the impression that remains
uppermost in our minds today: the subtle sense of Utopia.

Obviously, neither in a film nor in a book, nor in any way,
can one re-create such a special feeling. We recognized that it
was impossible to deal with 1968 head-on, squarely and directly.
But it occurred to Louis to inject a trace of what were called 'les
événements' ('the events') into the confines of a family story –
confined in space to a provincial household, and in time to a few
unpredictable days – and to make them play a role in the story.
And suddenly, to our surprise, this 'trace' of May '68 took on in

the script a presence, a truth, a strength, and a comic force –
the effects of which were instantly visible on the face of our
characters.

This simple geographical distancing, which is not dissimilar
to what Lévi-Strauss calls in anthropology 'the detached look',
can give that small breathing space which allows us to hear
better and even see better what isn't shown (because it cannot
be shown). The delicate dimensions of that breathing space are
difficult to establish and even more difficult to maintain: it is
important not to be too remote lest we become indifferent nor
too close, for that would make us partial.

Milou in May is obviously not a film about the student and
social unrest of May 1968. But without that unrest, the film
would have no resonance. It would simply be a banal story of
family squabbles, which we would never have written. It is the
remote echo of the Paris barricades – so often misinterpreted by
the characters – which takes them to the edge, to the limits of
their own selves. Although history often seems no more than a
fiction, it can sometimes stir in us the most powerful of our
dreams, our joys, our desires, and our fears.

Jean-Claude Carrière
(Trans. Pierre Hodgson)

Milou in May was first shown at the Curzon Mayfair, London, in 1990. The cast was as follows:

LÉONCE	Marcel Bories
MILOU	Michel Piccoli
CAMILLE	Miou-Miou
GEORGES	Michel Duchaussoy
CLAIRE	Dominique Blanc
LILY	Harriet Walter
GRIMALDI	Bruno Carette
MME VIEUZAC	Paulette Dubost
FRANÇOISE	Jeanne Hrry-Leclerc
ADÈLE	Martine Gautier
PAUL	Hubert Saint-Macary
DANIEL	François Berleand
MARIE-LAURE	Rozenn Le Tallec

Director of Photography	Renato Berta
Art Director	Willy Holt
Costumes	Catherine Leterrier
Editor	Emmanuelle Castro
Sound	Jean-Claude Laureux
Stills	Jeanne-Louise Bulliard
Music	Stephane Grappelli
Script	Louis Malle and Jean-Claude Carrière
Executive Producer	Vincent Malle
Producer and Director	Louis Malle

Mme Vieuzac
crying of
radio news
no
=
cutting onions

A wood of chestnut trees. LÉONCE, *eighty-two, spare and small-bodied, is standing under a swarm of bees, which envelops the crown of his head. Hundreds of bees cluster on his face.*
Next to him is a man, in gloves and mask, holding a book, and reading Virgil's Georgics *aloud to the bees. He is Emile Vieuzac, sixty, and is known as* MILOU.

MILOU: His quidam signis atque haec exempla secuti esse
    apibus partem divinae mentis et haustus aetherios
    dixere . . .

LÉONCE: Louder, Milou. Otherwise they can't hear you.
    (MILOU *turns a page of the book with his gloved hand.*)

MILOU: Uncle Albert used to say 'the only way to calm bees
    down is a bit of Virgil'.

LÉONCE: Yes, but dialect works as well . . . with bees from
    round here, anyway . . .
    (*In the distance a storm rumbles. Agitated, the bees start flying around.* MILOU *begins reading again.*)

The handsome face of a woman in her eighties. Huge tears run down her cheeks.
A news bulletin is heard on the radio:

RADIO: The strike is spreading all over the country. All public
    services are grinding to a halt. Several million workers are
    on strike. It's no longer possible to travel in France without
    a private car, and petrol stocks are running low. In Paris,
    people are queuing in food shops and stocking up on
    essentials such as coffee and sugar.
    (*The camera has pulled back slowly to reveal* MILOU'*s mother,*
    MME VIEUZAC, *peeling onions, in an old-fashioned country kitchen. A cat wanders along the kitchen counter.*)
Another violent demonstration took place last night in the
Latin Quarter. Student organizers were unable to prevent
confrontations which left twelve members of the police
injured. Fifty demonstrators were arrested. The National
Union of Students has denounced several cases of police
brutality. The prefect of police confirmed that the students

are now reinforced by armed militia. In the regions, farm labourers have built barricades around the town of Nantes. (MME VIEUZAC *puts the onions into the pan with a little oil.*) All political parties are waiting for a statement from General de Gaulle. Monsieur François Mitterrand has confirmed that if the government resigns he's ready to assume office. And now for a commercial break . . . (*Suddenly,* MME VIEUZAC *staggers, as if her legs have given way. She sits down for a moment, then gets up and, leaning against the wall for support, goes through into the hallway. She tries to cry out.*)

MME VIEUZAC: Adèle! . . . Milou! . . .

The ground floor of a large country house, furnished in late-nineteenth-century style. At the back of the dining room we glimpse a drawing room, in which the furniture is covered with dust sheets.
MME VIEUZAC, *leaning on the banister of the staircase, loosens her bodice. A song comes to her lips. She sings: 'Oh, your song is so pretty', she said, 'sing me another. Here, take these coins and teach me how' . . . tra la la la, tra la la . . .'*
She climbs a dozen or so steps, singing softly. A death-rattle sound;

*she collapses on to a sofa on the landing, lying amid several dolls
dressed in ballgowns. Her mouth gapes open.
The cat comes up and nuzzles her face.*
ADÈLE, *the housemaid, runs down the stairs.*

In the wood, LÉONCE, *assisted by* MILOU, *carefully breaks off the
branch from which the swarm is hanging and shakes it out on to the
ground in front of a small open hive.*
LÉONCE: They're really nervous this year.
MILOU: Well, it's in the air.
   (*The bees are now going into the hive, in regular lines.* MILOU
   takes off his mask and smiles at LÉONCE, *who says a few
   words in dialect to the bees.*
   A voice is heard in the distance.)
ADÈLE (*Voice over*) Monsieur Vieuzac! Monsieur Vieuzac!
MILOU: I'm late for lunch. Mother will be mad at me.
LÉONCE: Go on, then, I'll finish this. But don't run.
   (MILOU *moves away, taking small steps, eyes on the bees.*
   After a few yards, he gets his bicycle and rides off bumpily.)

Credits over: MILOU *riding his bike through the woods, then
through a field of poppies, and finally approaching a beautiful ivy-*

3

covered house. Passing under a cherry tree, he grabs a handful of cherries and goes into the house, wheeling his bike in with him.

MME VIEUZAC's *face. A strong peasant hand is liberally applying make-up to her cheeks and lips. The dead woman's mouth is half open.*
She has been laid out on a narrow bed, a rosary between her fingers; she's dressed in a severe black suit and silk blouse, as if she were going to mass. Two lit candles and a crucifix are at the head of the bed.
ADÈLE *is now arranging the dead woman's hair.* ADÈLE *is twenty-eight, with an almost palpable sensuality about her.*
MILOU's *voice is heard as he telephones, along with the operator's, which is unintelligible but audibly exasperated.*
MILOU: Mademoiselle, you promised me half an hour ago you'd get that number in London . . . What? Of course it's urgent! My poor mother has just died . . . Thank you, you're very kind . . . And what about Nice? Can you get me Nice? . . . I know, I know, but it's not my fault if your colleagues are on strike! . . . Don't shout at me, I'm just trying to call my family.

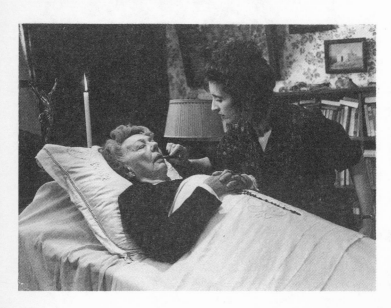

(LÉONCE, *at the foot of the bed, watches over the dead woman.*
In the hallway, MILOU *continues to shout himself hoarse on the phone, speaking now in appalling English.*)
Allo! Allo! . . . Mister Vieuzac, please, for his brother . . .
He is not here? You know where I can touch him? . . .
Wait a moment, I write the number . . .
(*On the wall behind* MILOU *is a large photograph taken at the turn of the century. A zebra is attached to a carriage in front of the Vieuzac house. A man bearing a strong resemblance to* MILOU *stands next to the zebra.*
The parish PRIEST, *a big, solidly built man under his surplice, comes into the house.* MILOU *points to the library.*)
She's in there . . . I'm just coming.

In the library, the PRIEST *is giving the blessing, with* MILOU, ADÈLE *and* LÉONCE *in attendance. A news bulletin is barely audible on the radio, an old Bakelite set on a small round table. The* PRIEST *cocks an ear and, while continuing his prayers for the dead, steps to the side and turns the volume up in order to hear the live broadcast: a reporter at the scene of a student demonstration.*
PRIEST: (*Taking off his surplice*) Did you hear that? They've organized a hospital at the Sorbonne . . . Yes, the medical students. It's all working like clockwork, apparently.
MILOU: Right now you don't see much of God on the barricades, monsieur le curé.
PRIEST: That's because people don't know how to look, Monsieur Vieuzac.
MILOU: Maybe.

MILOU *is eating alone at the big table in the dining room, a large towel round his shoulders.* ADÈLE *is cutting his hair.*
ADÈLE: Keep still. I don't want you looking like a savage at the cemetery.
MILOU: Were you able to find any chicken?
ADÈLE: Yes . . . and some cheese. It's bread that's going to be difficult. I've got some unsalted biscuits.
(ADÈLE *steps back to look at* MILOU's *hair.*)
There, that's much neater . . . Now, eat! If she saw you

like this, she'd be really upset. (*She makes for the kitchen.*) Did you get through to Camille?

MILOU: Yes, she'll be here tomorrow.

ADÈLE: And what about Claire?

MILOU: Claire too.

ADÈLE: And Georges?

MILOU: He's in Saint-Tropez. Can you believe it! What on earth can he be doing there?

(*He stands and picks up a fur wrap draped over a piece of furniture, goes into the kitchen and puts it around* ADÈLE's *shoulders.*)

Here, before they arrive, I'm giving you her fox fur, as a present. Do you like it?

ADÈLE: I'd never dare wear it, it's too fine.

(*From behind, he takes her in his arms, and kisses her neck, insistently, almost desperately. She disengages herself, taking off the fur.*)

No, not tonight, not with death in the house, it's bad luck. Anyway, I've got my period.

(MILOU *moves away, grumbling.*)

You're tired, go and lie down. I'll stay here with her. I'll wake you up when I leave.

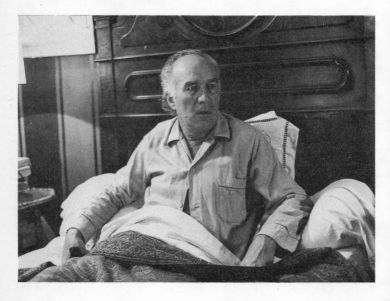

(*Watched by* ADÈLE, MILOU *goes up the stairs with his bicycle.*)

MILOU *comes into the bedroom, props up his bicycle, then opens the window. He takes off his shoes and puts them in a cupboard, in which dozens of rather battered pairs are lined up.*
He sits in bed in his pyjamas, staring fixedly. There is the sound of an owl hooting, coming closer and closer.
Tears run down his face and his body is racked with sobs.
He turns his head and sees the owl sitting on the window-ledge, looking at him.

*A Citroën DS19 is driving along a road parallel to some factory buildings on the outskirts of a small town. An enormous banner, '*BOUTELLEAU'S ON STRIKE*'; some red flags. The 'Internationale' is heard.*
In front of of the factory gates, strikers force the car to slow down, holding out pamphlets to the driver. Everyone is quite well behaved. There are a few policemen, with rifles slung over their shoulders.

Inside the Citroën there is a family: PAUL *drives;* CAMILLE *sits next to him. Behind,* FRANÇOISE, *aged ten, her nose stuck up*

against the window. Two small boys, twins, sleep in each other's arms on the back seat.

CAMILLE: Look at them. Any excuse to take it easy.

PAUL: Don't provoke them.

CAMILLE: Boutelleau can't be too happy.

PAUL: Serves him right.

> (CAMILLE *has a basket on her lap, and a Hermès scarf round her neck. She's thirty-five and always talks very quickly. A* YOUNG WORKER *offers her a pamphlet.*)

YOUNG WORKER: Here, something for you to read, comrade.

CAMILLE: Thank you.

> (*She smiles at the striker as she takes the pamphlet. He moves away.* PAUL *whistles the 'Internationale' mechanically.*)
> Paul!

PAUL: Oh! Sorry . . .

In front of the house, MILOU *is repairing his bike as he discusses arrangements for the burial with* M. DELMAS, *a small jovial man in a black suit, who is going through the pages of a catalogue.*

DELMAS: This one is in oak, silk-lined, copper handles, not too ornate. That's what they chose for Madame de Villecelles, last year. And it's a very reasonable price.

> (MILOU *looks at the catalogue.*)

MILOU: You're right, very tasteful.

DELMAS: And elegant. That's the one I'd recommend. If I order it now, it'll be ready for tomorrow.

> (*A tile falls from the roof, and breaks at their feet.* DELMAS *jumps back, startled.* MILOU *pushes at the pieces with his foot.*)

MILOU: And what about petrol?

DELMAS: I'm still waiting. All the petrol pumps have been drained dry. Malaval the grocer has filled his bathtub! If they're ever hit by lightning . . . !

MILOU: You don't have a horse-drawn hearse any more?

DELMAS: Not for the last ten years! If it goes on like this, those horses will be sorely missed. Is the vault ready?

MILOU: I'm going to go and check today.

The Citroën drives through the vineyard and approaches the grounds.

CAMILLE: (*To the children*) Do you want some biscuits?

PAUL: What are all of you planning to do with the house?
CAMILLE: Well, the best thing would be to sell it, if we can get
Father to agree. Why, do you want it?
PAUL: Too much of a burden.
FRANÇOISE: But what about our holidays?
CAMILLE: We'll go to the seaside. It's very bracing.
FRANÇOISE: Oh no, not the seaside! We're better off here.
CAMILLE: Be quiet, Françoise.

The Citroën draws up in front of the entrance to the house. MILOU
runs out to welcome them, kisses CAMILLE.
CAMILLE: Poor Daddy . . . Was it you who found her? It must
have been a shock . . .
(MILOU *takes the children in his arms.*)
MILOU: Ah, the twins . . .
CAMILLE: Who knows, it could have been the revolution that
killed her . . . she always hated disorder.
(FRANÇOISE *throws herself round her grandfather's neck.*
CAMILLE *takes several bags from the boot of the car.*)
I've brought two kilos of sugar – I'm sure you didn't think
to buy any. And flour. It always comes in handy. And some
oil. Where's Adèle?
MILOU: She's making up the rooms.
PAUL: In Bordeaux, all the shops are shutting down.
CAMILLE: All because of those idiots at the Sorbonne.
PAUL: Spoilt brats . . .
MILOU: They're managing pretty well, though, aren't they?
CAMILLE: What they need is their heads knocked together.
Maybe even a death or two. By the way, have you put her
in the drawing room?
MILOU: In the library.
(*Still talking, they go into the house, carrying the groceries and
the luggage. Suddenly realizing he hasn't greeted his son-in-
law,* MILOU *shakes hands with him in the doorway.*)

*In the library, a moment of reflection before the deceased. They
sprinkle her with holy water using a palm frond.*
*The children stand directly in front of the body and stare, bursting
with curiosity.*

CAMILLE: You were right to put her in here . . . She looks so peaceful . . .

MILOU: Yes, for once in her life.

PAUL: When is the funeral?

MILOU: The day after tomorrow, if everyone's here by then.

PAUL: Do you want me to call in on the solicitor on the way back?

CAMILLE: You're going back?

PAUL: I can't spend two days here. I'll leave and come back.

CAMILLE: What have you got to do in Bordeaux that's so urgent?

PAUL: The sick don't go on strike, you know.

(FRANÇOISE *has gone over to the body.*)

FRANÇOISE: Is it all right to kiss her?

CAMILLE: No, it's too late now. Say a prayer.

At the cemetery, the Vieuzac vault is open. MILOU *is leaning over* LÉONCE, *whose head is barely visible above the edge of the tomb.*

LÉONCE: Best to put her on this side. It's not as damp.

MILOU: Is that Father there?

LÉONCE: Yes.

(LÉONCE *taps a rather dilapidated coffin with the flat of his hand.*)

There can't be much left of him. Wood always lasts longer than bones. Have you thought about the flowers yet?

MILOU: No.

LÉONCE: I'll see to it.

CAMILLE *is at the kitchen window, chasing flies with a Flytox pump.*

CAMILLE: Come on kids, time to eat!

(*She hears the sound of a car, leans over to take a look. Outside, a red convertible Alfa-Romeo brakes sharply. It is* DANIEL PONS, *the solicitor from Romagne. He keeps the motor running, and jumps out of the car without opening the door.*

In the kitchen CAMILLE *smiles and goes to the oven to take out a crème brûlée.*

FRANÇOISE *and the twins burst into the kitchen, bumping into* DANIEL *in the doorway. They sit down at the table.*)

Have you washed your hands? Oh, it's you, Daniel . . .
(*They kiss, rather awkwardly.* CAMILLE *holds the dish with a cloth.* DANIEL *burns himself.*)

DANIEL: Ouch!

CAMILLE: Watch out! It's hot.

DANIEL: I'm awfully sorry about your grandmother. I was very fond of her.

CAMILLE: Thank you. It's all been so sudden.
(CAMILLE *dips a finger into the crême brûlée to taste it, which she does several times.*)

DANIEL: I see you haven't lost your appetite, though.

CAMILLE: What, me? I hardly eat anything. Got yourself a new car, then?

DANIEL: Yes, an Alfa-Romeo. Delicate but very highly strung.

CAMILLE: Business going well?

DANIEL: Not bad, up until last month. At the moment, though, it's hard to say how things will turn out.
(*They lower their voices.* FRANÇOISE *pricks up her ears.*)
If you decide to sell the house, let me know. I could be of some help.

CAMILLE: Does Father still owe you money?

DANIEL: Of course.

CAMILLE: How much?
(*With his fingers* DANIEL *indicates a figure.*)
Seven?
(DANIEL *nods.*)

DANIEL: I'll come over and read the will once Georges and Claire have arrived.

CAMILLE: Any surprises?

DANIEL: Oh no, the usual. Three heirs, three shares.

CAMILLE: So I don't get anything.

DANIEL: Not now. But you're the only child, you'll inherit your father's share.
(*As he talks, he puts his hand on her hip. She moves away.* FRANÇOISE *watches them as she eats her soup.*)
Still ticklish?

CAMILLE: It depends. And what about you? Still not married?

DANIEL: No, I'm waiting for you.

CAMILLE: How d'you manage, in the meantime?

DANIEL: Oh, you know, these days, with the Pill . . .

CAMILLE: Even here in the countryside?
DANIEL: Even here.

It's evening. The library. CAMILLE, MILOU *and* FRANÇOISE
watch over MME VIEUZAC. CAMILLE *gets up, yawning.*
CAMILLE: I'm going to bed, I'm dead on my feet. Are you
　　coming, Françoise?
FRANÇOISE: I'll stay here with Grandad.
　　(CAMILLE *kisses her father and goes out.* FRANÇOISE *leans
　　over to* MILOU, *who's dozing.*)
　　Grandad . . .
MILOU: Yes?
FRANÇOISE: What's the Pill?
MILOU: It's progress, that's what.

*A road in the middle of a forest. The deep silence is punctuated by
night birds calling to one another.*
A 2CV is parked. A young woman, CLAIRE, *leans against the car,
her face drawn and tense. She is twenty-eight, with a beautiful
though severe face. No make-up. She jumps at a rustling sound
behind her.*
*Suddenly, the sound of a scooter, which then appears round the
bend, driven by a young man with a very young woman,* MARIE-
LAURE, *perched behind him, clutching a petrol can.*
MARIE-LAURE: Weren't you frightened?
CLAIRE: Of course not! Afraid of what?
　　(*The* YOUNG MAN *fills the 2CV's tank. As he chats, he keeps
　　making clucking noises with his mouth.*)
YOUNG MAN: That's the trouble with 2CVs; you always think
　　there's some petrol left and then they break down on you
　　just like any other car. I've given you some of the petrol I'd
　　been saving for myself. Only because she turned on the
　　charm.
CLAIRE: How much do I owe you?
YOUNG MAN: Five francs. I won't charge you the call out fee.
　　(*Whilst* CLAIRE *pays him,* MARIE-LAURE *gets in the driving
　　seat.* CLAIRE *gets in next to her. The* YOUNG MAN *leans over
　　to* MARIE-LAURE *and asks:*)
　　No kiss goodbye?

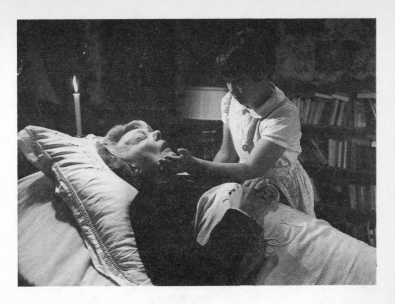

(MARIE-LAURE *puts two fingers to her lips, kisses them, then places the kiss on the* YOUNG MAN'*s cheek.*)
CLAIRE: Come on, let's go.

In the library, MILOU *is snoring.* FRANÇOISE *gets up, and walks around* MME VIEUZAC. *She climbs on to a stool and leans over the dead woman's face to kiss her. She whispers:*
FRANÇOISE: Grandma . . . It's me, Françoise. Are you in
heaven . . . or in hell? If you're in hell, blink your eye.
(*No response.* FRANÇOISE *strokes her grandmother's cheek, then starts to slap her, gently but firmly, as if to wake her up.*)
Close your mouth, Grandma, or you'll get dirt in it.
(*She tries to lift her chin.*
The cat climbs on to the bed and looks on, mewing.
MILOU *mutters something, opens his eyes. He sees* FRANÇOISE *from behind, leaning over the body. Her short skirt reveals the tops of her thighs.* MILOU *watches her, smiling.* FRANÇOISE *traces the outline of her grandmother's nose, pinches her earlobe. She puts a finger up one of her nostrils. She turns round.* MILOU *shuts his eyes again.*)

The landing. CAMILLE, *in pyjamas, slips into Mme Vieuzac's*

13

*bedroom. Without putting the light on, she goes straight over to the
bureau, raises the lid, and opens an antique box with a quilted
lining. The glint of jewellery. We see* CAMILLE's *hand take an
emerald ring, which she slips on to her finger.
She hears the sound of a 2CV approaching. Quickly she puts the
jewellery box back in its place.*

The hallway. MILOU, *carrying a sleeping* FRANÇOISE *in his arms,
goes to meet* CLAIRE *and* MARIE-LAURE, *who are carrying
identical bags.*
CLAIRE *is limping slightly.* MILOU *kisses her.*
MILOU: My dear little Claire . . . you're a grown woman now
. . . and mademoiselle?
CLAIRE: My uncle, Emile Vieuzac . . . Marie-Laure Mounier.
She's on her way to visit her parents in Angoulême. Can
you put her up for the night?
MILOU: Of course.
(CLAIRE *looks at* FRANÇOISE.)
CLAIRE: Who's that?
MILOU: Françoise, Camille's daughter.
CLAIRE: Oh, really.
MILOU: You don't mind having to share a room?
MARIE-LAURE: Not at all.
MILOU: The buttercup room. Do you remember? It was Aunt
Zette's bedroom.
(*He puts his bike on his shoulder and starts up the stairs taking*
FRANÇOISE *by the hand. He turns round to point towards the
library.*)
Mother's in there. If you're hungry, Camille has made her
a cake.
(MARIE-LAURE *is extending her leg backwards in a ballet
movement. She comes up to* CLAIRE.)
MARIE-LAURE: Is that one of your mother's brothers?
CLAIRE: Yes, the eldest.
MARIE-LAURE: What does he do?
CLAIRE: Nothing. Looks after the property. Or so he says. He's
all right. Come on.
MARIE-LAURE: You go on in without me.
CLAIRE: Why?
MARIE-LAURE: I've never seen a dead person close up.

CLAIRE: All the more reason. Come on.
  (*She drags her in to the library, taking her right up to Mme Vieuzac's bed.*)
  She's aged.
MARIE-LAURE: Don't you feel anything at all?
CLAIRE: I didn't like her. She used to make me wash my hands at least four times a day. After the accident, I couldn't run or swim any more, but she used to keep nagging, 'Come on, make an effort, get a move on, you're always trailing behind the others. And what about the piano? I haven't heard you practising today.'
MARIE-LAURE: Where did the accident happen?
CLAIRE: On the way here. My father had been drinking. He missed a bend. I was stuck for three hours in the wreckage. They both died, him and my mother. I was eight years old.
MARIE-LAURE: Is that why you don't drive? (*She leans over the body.*) You look a little bit like her, you know.
  (CLAIRE *looks at her, surprised, then takes another look at the dead woman.*)

Late morning. In front of the house the twins are perched astride an old donkey, which MILOU *leads by the reins.*
LÉONCE *comes up, with two large wreaths of flowers which he leaves at the entrance of the house. His dog, a big mountain sheepdog, follows him like a shadow.*
In the kitchen, CAMILLE *and* ADÈLE *are making an enormous* pot-au-feu. ADÈLE *notices Mme Vieuzac's emerald ring on* CAMILLE'*s finger, but doesn't say anything.*
CAMILLE: Are these all the carrots they had?
ADÈLE: It's not my fault! Everyone was after vegetables . . .
  Madame Calvignac had half a ton of potatoes delivered to her house.
CAMILLE: Half a tone? They'll start sprouting before she gets through them!
  (FRANÇOISE, *in her night-dress, comes bounding down the stairs, four at a time. She comes in to the kitchen.*)
  Do you know what time it is?
  (FRANÇOISE *swipes a piece of toast, smears jam on it.*)
ADÈLE: How many places should I lay the table for?
CAMILLE: Ten, maybe twelve. You never know.

ADÈLE: I took the only meat that was left, apparently there just isn't any more around. Everything's come to a standstill – the trains, the post . . .

CAMILLE: Even with Pompidou caving in to all their demands! Thirty per cent! What more can they ask for? No, not those plates! Use Aunt Zette's.

(*Annoyed,* ADÈLE *comes back with her pile of plates.*)

ADÈLE: Well, I think I ought to go on strike myself. When I worked it out, I don't even get the SMIG.* You don't want me to put out the crystal glasses, do you? They'll break.

FRANÇOISE: What's the SMIG?

CAMILLE: Go and get dressed, and wake up your Aunt Claire. She's in the buttercup room.

FRANÇOISE: I know.

(*She takes her toast and goes out as quickly as she came in.*)

ADÈLE: It must be at least ten years since we last saw Mademoiselle Claire.

CAMILLE: Yes, it took a death in the family to get her here.

ADÈLE: I wonder if she's still as odd as she used to be? She's supposed to be an antique dealer, isn't she?

* Salaire minimum interprofessionel garanti, i.e. minimum wage.

(MILOU *and the twins on the donkey go past the window. They wave at* CAMILLE.)

On the landing. FRANÇOISE *knocks, then opens the door into the buttercup room. The two women, in twin beds, are asleep:* CLAIRE *buried under the bedclothes,* MARIE-LAURE *on her back, naked, her upper body exposed. One of her wrists is attached to the bedpost by a small piece of rope.*
Still munching her toast, FRANÇOISE *looks at her.*
MILOU'*s voice is heard outside.*
MILOU: But what on earth happened to you? Where's the car?
  (FRANÇOISE *goes to open the window, and sees Milou's younger brother* GEORGES *entering the grounds, with his wife* LILY *a few yards behind. They're on foot, carrying leather suitcases.* GEORGES *quickens his pace,* LILY *trails behind.* MILOU *leads the donkey with the twins towards them.*)

GEORGES *puts his case down in the hallway. He's wearing a summer jacket and an Ascot; he's forty-five to fifty, a Parisian intellectual.* CAMILLE *comes out of the kitchen.*
CAMILLE: Georges! You didn't walk all the way from Saint-Tropez?
GEORGES: We ran out of petrol at the level crossing. Is the radio working?
  (*Without waiting for an answer, he goes into the library and switches the radio on, ignoring his mother's body.* LILY *and* MILOU *come in to the hallway,* MILOU *carrying the luggage.* LILY *collapses on to a trunk. She's nearing forty, and is very pretty. She speaks French with an English accent. She's wearing one of those Afghan coats which were all the rage at the time.*)
LILY: Hello, Camille.
CAMILLE: Hello, Lily.
  (*She holds her arms up as she kisses her.*)
  Excuse my hands, they're oily.
LILY: Not a drop of petrol all the way from Saint-Tropez. (*In English*) A nightmare.
  (FRANÇOISE *rushes down the stairs and comes to kiss her.*)
FRANÇOISE: Nice coat.

MILOU: Yes, it's nice, though you can still smell the goat. I'll
take it.
(*He helps* LILY *out of her coat, adding*:)
Ah, that lovely English neck . . .
LILY: I'm the one that smells like a goat! We were driving all
night. It was simply impossible to get a wink of sleep.
Georges was getting all worked up because the radio . . . Is
it really that serious, what's happening in Paris?
MILOU: Georges is the one who decides what's serious or not.

In the library, GEORGES *is listening to a live broadcast: a very
noisy demonstration in the Latin Quarter.* MILOU *comes up behind
him and turns the volume down.*
MILOU: Don't you want to see Mother?
(GEORGES *turns and throws his arms round his brother.*
MILOU *leads him over to their mother's body.* GEORGES
weeps.
LILY *comes into the room, strokes a rhinoceros head hanging on
the wall, then approaches the body. The two brothers compose
themselves. But it's clear from* GEORGES'S *face that he's still
listening to the radio broadcast.*
LILY *pinches him. He jumps, leans towards her.*)
GEORGES: Remind me to call the paper. They must be
wondering where I am.
(*He takes the palm frond, makes the sign of the cross with it,
and hands it to* LILY.
*She looks at it, sniffs it. Not knowing what it's for, she throws
it away behind her.*)

MILOU, GEORGES, LILY, C⟨...⟩ARIE-LAURE, FRANÇOISE
and the twins are sitting roun⟨...⟩ in the dining room.
CAMILLE *and* ADÈLE *serve ⟨...⟩-au-feu: a large plate of
mixed meats, a tureen of broth⟨...⟩ dishes of vegetables, along
with gherkins, rock salt, must⟨...⟩ey talk, food is constantly
passed round, plates held out,⟨...⟩hanged.*
The children eat and listen, as⟨...⟩a show. CLAIRE *examines
the silver.* GEORGES *is holding⟨...⟩*
GEORGES: But is the Commu⟨...⟩ready to embark on such
a venture? (*In English*) '⟨...⟩question.' (*In French*)
For the time being, the s⟨...⟩still spontaneous, and

[Handwritten note overlaid: "when she throws it away Georges + Milou give her a bitchy/unbelievable look"]

localized. It all lacks co-ordination. And without a really
big workers' movement, no revolution is possible. Just as
Marx said. The left is trying to jump on the bandwagon,
without really having any idea of where it's heading . . .
Could you pass me a little bit of bone marrow?
(MILOU, *sitting next to him, serves him some.*)
And it's obvious that the government were taken
completely by surprise. Completely! They underestimated
the students, de Gaulle more than anyone else. And now
they're floundering! Simply floundering!

CAMILLE: They ought to bring in the army!

GEORGES: It's not so simple! It's an absolute miracle that so far
nobody's been killed!

CLAIRE: Apparently there have been some deaths, but they hide
the bodies at night! Could you pass me the salt?

GEORGES: The real danger, my dear Claire, lies in whether the
movement gains mass support – then there'll be real
trouble. If so, folks, (*in English*) 'what a mess'!
(MILOU *spreads some bone marrow on a piece of bread.*)

MILOU: D'you think it could go that far? Really?

CAMILLE: Come off it! A firm hand is all that's needed, then
it'll be over in no time! Nobody in France wants
revolution!

GEORGES: Well, Camille, that's what people were saying in
1789, only a month before they stormed the Bastille.
(MILOU *drops a bit of bone marrow on his shirt.*)

MILOU: Arghhh! It always happens to me . . .

GEORGES: You've alw~~ays been a m~~essy eater.

MILOU: And what abc ~~ut your~~ ~~br~~ain?

GEORGES: What?

MILOU: Your son? Di~~d you~~ know?

GEORGES: I left a mes~~sage~~ He's impossible to get hold
of.

CAMILLE: He's far too ~~busy~~ ~~h~~aving stones and
throwing them at ~~the police~~

(*One of the twins th~~rows a bit of f~~ ~~bread, hitt~~ing MARIE-
LAURE *on the foreh~~ead~~*)

GEORGES: Could you p~~ass me the g~~erk~~i~~ns.

MARIE-LAURE: Are you ~~.~~

GEORGES: Yes, I've been *Le Monde*'s London correspondent for eleven years now.

MILOU: What were you up to in Saint-Tropez?

GEORGES: I'm on leave. Le Seuil are publishing a book of mine in November. But I haven't finished it yet.

MILOU: A book about what?

GEORGES: Gaullism. I'm still looking for a title. *The Rupture*, perhaps. What d'you think?

MILOU: Not bad. The rupture with what?

GEORGES: My dear chap, what's happening now proves everything I'm saying in the book. No provision's been made for the young! Nothing at all! By the way, when's the funeral?

(MILOU *turns his back on* GEORGES, *fixing his eyes on* LILY.)

MILOU: Tomorrow. What a beautiful sight, a woman eating.

GEORGES: I have to get back to Paris as soon as possible. Can you get *Le Monde* round here?

MILOU: I don't know.

(*He pours a glass of wine for* LILY.)

Try the '64. It's got a fresh young taste.

GEORGES: It's really annoying, not being able to get hold of *Le Monde*. Particularly at the moment.

(MARIE-LAURE *throws a bread pellet at the twins, then turns to* LILY.)

MARIE-LAURE: And you, madame, what do you do?

LILY: Nothing.

GEORGES: Don't talk like that, Lily! You're an actress.

LILY: I'm an actress, but I'm not doing anything.

(CAMILLE *offers* CLAIRE *some vegetables*.)

CAMILLE: Would you like some carrots?

(CLAIRE *sees the ring on* CAMILLE's *finger*.)

CLAIRE: That's grandmother's emerald.

CAMILLE: Yes, she gave it to me two years ago.

CLAIRE: Ah . . .

CAMILLE: As we're all here, we ought to decide what we're going to do.

GEORGES: You mean: what we're going to do about dividing up the inheritance?

CAMILLE: Exactly.

GEORGES: I've been giving it some thought. There's three of us.

We could divide things up three ways: the vineyard, the house, and the Corot . . . By the way . . . where is the Corot?
(*He looks up at the wall.*
CLAIRE *turns round. We see a rectangular shape on the wall, paler than the surrounding wallpaper.*)
MILOU: It was sold three years ago.
GEORGES: The Corot's been sold?
MILOU: Yes. The roof had to be repaired.
CLAIRE: And you sold it?
MILOU: Yes, through an antique dealer in Bordeaux, a friend of Camille's.
CLAIRE: No doubt you were cheated.
MILOU: No doubt. But if you'd replied to my letter . . .
GEORGES: You could have talked to me first, for Christ's sake!
CLAIRE: If there's only the house and the land, it's going to be difficult to split three ways.
CAMILLE: Unless we sell.
MILOU: We sell what?
CAMILLE: The house and the land. Then we'd share the money, it's far simpler that way. The money and the furniture.

GEORGES: I've no objections. (*To* LILY *in English*) We could use the money.

MILOU: You'd actually sell the house?

CLAIRE: Why not?

MILOU: But this house is the only thing that keeps us all together! We'd be nothing without the house. No better than gypsies, no roots, nothing!

GEORGES: Listen, Milou, it's all very well your staying here, but without the vineyard, what would you live on?

CAMILLE: You've never earned a penny in your life!

(*A moment of embarrassment.* LILY *intervenes:*)

LILY: But how would you share out the furniture?

CAMILLE: The usual way. You make a three-way split, of roughly equal value, and then draw lots. We can swamp among ourselves afterwards.

(*Outside, two women – neighbours – peer in through the dining-room window.*)

LILY: Is that how you do it? Draw lots?

CAMILLE: Yes, always. We could even make a start today. It wouldn't take long.

MILOU: You want to start dividing up the furniture today. With Mother here?

CAMILLE: Of course! Since we're all here together for once! Georges is going away tomorrow, and Claire as well . . . I assume you don't really care about the house, Claire, since you never come here anyway! You'd only be interested in the furniture.

(CLAIRE *turns to her, very annoyed.*)

CLAIRE: Why should you decide everything? Your father's the one who inherits, not you! You don't have any right to anything!

MILOU: But why do you want to sell everything? You're all mad! The vineyard, if necessary, since it isn't worth much any more. But let's keep the house, so you can all keep coming here for the holidays! Like you always have!

(*He throws down his napkin.*)

Dammit, I've lost my appetite! I want to die in this house. It's my right! I'm telling you, you're not going to take my childhood away from me!

(*He gets up and goes off to the kitchen. We hear him shout something at* ADÈLE.

A door slams.

Meanwhile, the two neighbours have appeared in the dining-room doorway.)

FIRST NEIGHBOUR: My dear Camille . . .

(CAMILLE *jumps up, then gestures to the others.*)

CAMILLE: I'll go.

SECOND NEIGHBOUR: And to go on Mother's Day . . .

(CAMILLE *ushers them towards the library.*)

CAMILLE: She's in there . . .

FIRST NEIGHBOUR: It must have taken her by surprise, dying like that. She was always a planner.

SECOND NEIGHBOUR: Believe you me, she's better up there with everything that's going on . . . Paris in flames and bloodshed everywhere . . .

(*They disappear. The cat has taken the opportunity to jump on to the table in the dining room.* LILY *catches hold of her and strokes her.*)

LILY: You're lucky. In Egypt, they'd have buried you with her.

MILOU'*s bike is leaning against a tree.*

Alone, MILOU *is undressing, on the bank of a little river at the*

bottom of the grounds. Rather ominously, he takes off his shirt and his shoes. It looks as though he's about to throw himself in the water. A voice is heard: 'Grandad! Grandad! Wait for me!'
MILOU *straightens up.*
FRANÇOISE *comes running up. They look at each other without exchanging a word. He gets into the water.*
FRANÇOISE: Grandad, why do you keep your trousers on?
MILOU: So I don't catch cold.
(*The water's now up to his chest. He gropes with both arms under the riverbank, then crouches down. His face and hat are all that's visible.*)
FRANÇOISE: Will it work?
MILOU: Yes, they love it. They're mad for human flesh.
FRANÇOISE: Grandad, why does Aunt Claire tie her friend up?
MILOU: She ties her up?
FRANÇOISE: Yes. To the bed.
MILOU: Well, probably so she won't go away. Shhh, be quiet, I can feel them . . .
(FRANÇOISE *kneels down and leans over.* MILOU *is shivering.* LILY *appears, a magnificent Indian shawl around her shoulders. She's smoking a joint.*)
LILY: What are you doing?
(FRANÇOISE *turns round and goes, 'Shush.'*
MILOU *grimaces with pain, then suddenly pulls his hands out of the water, with five or six crayfish hanging from his fingers.* FRANÇOISE *claps.*)
(*In English*) Incredible!
MILOU: Françoise! Quickly, the bag!

In the dining room, the table has been extended and now stretches from one wall to the other. CAMILLE, ADÈLE *and* MARIE-LAURE *are putting piles of plates on it. The twins are running around the table.* CAMILLE *chases them away.*
CAMILLE: Stop getting in the way!
(*She joins* CLAIRE *in the hallway.*)
The simplest thing would be to start with the crockery. Then the silver . . . We can sort out the furniture later. What d'you think?
(*She looks at* CLAIRE, *who makes a face as she examines herself in the mirror.*)

24

That mirror isn't very flattering. The one over there is
better.

CLAIRE: Do you feel you're getting old?

CAMILLE: Me ~ ~
(CLAIRE ~ ~ ~ CAMILLE *is holding in her*
hand, and ~ *ng room.*)

CLAIRE: Wha ~ ~ ~?

CAMILLE: No ~ ~ last year, just in case . . . With
an antiqu ~ ~ nily, why should I need a
valuation? ~ ~

(CLAIRE ~ ~ *et covering the drawing-room*
furniture.)

CLAIRE: All th ~ ~ ch. There's only one good piece
of furnitu ~ ~

CAMILLE: Wh ~ ~

CLAIRE: You k ~ ~ ell.

CAMILLE: The ~ ~ board?

CLAIRE: The I ~ ~ ard! It's a fake!

CAMILLE: Are ~ ~

(*She looks* ~ ~ *uneasy, going through her papers.*
The twins ~ ~ *ursued by* ADÈLE.)

ADÈLE: Out! Now.

CLAIRE: Camille, please, get your kids out of here. They're
going to break everything.

CAMILLE: Go and play outside! Go on!
(*She goes out for a moment with the children.*)

CLAIRE: Adèle, did you know about the ring?

ADÈLE: What ring?

CLAIRE: The emerald. By rights, it should have gone to
Mother, then to me.
(CAMILLE *comes back into the room.*)

CAMILLE: Yes, but Grandmother gave it to me.

CLAIRE: That's what you say. (*To* ADÈLE) Did you know about
this?
(*Carrying a pile of plates,* ADÈLE *goes out of the room.*)

ADÈLE: Oh, they never talked to me about things like that.

The river. FRANÇOISE *hands the bag of crayfish to* MILOU *who*
shakes his fingers out and throws the last of his catch into the bag.

MILOU: When I was young, you could fill whole buckets with

them, and they were big ones too! If we meet a policeman, keep them out of sight. It's forbidden.

FRANÇOISE: Aren't they on strike?

MILOU: That's all we need!

(*He gets out of the water, blue with cold.*)

LILY: Don't you have a towel? (*In English*) You're mad!

(*She undoes her shawl and puts it round his shoulders, then rubs his back.*)

MILOU: (*Teeth chattering*) I couldn't live without the river . . . the trees. If they take it all away from me . . .

FRANÇOISE: Where's the shawl from?

LILY: Srinagar.

FRANÇOISE: Where's that?

LILY: It's in India.

FRANÇOISE: Have you been to India then?

LILY: Yes. Several times. I even dragged your Uncle Georges there. He got so sick!

(*They go back up to the house, through the trees,* MILOU *wheeling his bike along,* FRANÇOISE *carrying the bag of crayfish.*)

MILOU: I don't know how he does it, your Uncle Georges. He isn't particularly handsome, nor particularly clever. At school, I used to do better than him. But he always manages to come across the ideal woman, just like that.

FRANÇOISE: How did he meet you?

LILY: On a plane.

MILOU: On a plane. You see what I mean?

LILY: It was right above the Atlantic, during a terrible storm, lightning everywhere. The plane kept hitting air-pockets . . . People were screaming, it was awful! Georges had got up to go to the toilet . . . you know Georges . . . On the way back the plane was shaking so much that he fell over and ended up in the seat next to me! I was frightened, so I took hold of his hand, and that's how I came to be your aunt . . .

MILOU: Can you believe it! All because of a storm. He finds himself next to her. Lucky devil.

LILY: When it all calmed down, he talked to me about politics.

MILOU: Ah yes, that's Georges all over.

26

LILY: I just loved his French accent. He seemed so serious! . . .
    Ah, Milou . . . if I'd met you beforehand, who knows?
MILOU: It's a long time since I've been on a plane.
    (*Suddenly he gives a long, Tarzan-like cry.*)
LILY: What's that for?
MILOU: Shhh . . . The better to feel the silence.
    (*He sucks his fingertips.*)
LILY: You're bleeding!
MILOU: Combat wounds!

They're nearing the house. An outlandish sight greets them in front of the house: Georges's Rover, being pulled along by the donkey, led by LÉONCE. GEORGES *is walking along by the side of the car, manoeuvring the steering wheel and listening to the radio.*
LILY, FRANÇOISE *and* MILOU *emerge from the wood.* LILY *is perched on Milou's bike, with* MILOU *holding the saddle and handlebars.* LILY *cries out in alarm.*
MILOU: Take the handlebars! Just hold on to them! Right, I'm
    going to let go!
LILY: No! No!
    (*She loses her balance and grabs on to* MILOU, *hanging round his neck, laughing. She hears the radio and sees* GEORGES.)
    (*In English*) So what's new?
GEORGES: De Gaulle is going to speak tonight. It's about time.
    (*He moves away.* FRANÇOISE *turns to* LILY.)
FRANÇOISE: Do you like de Gaulle?
LILY: Not particularly.
FRANÇOISE: I knew it. The English don't like them.

In front of the house. A ladder is leaning against the cherry tree. The twins are perched in the branches, stuffing themselves with cherries. ADÈLE, *arms full, appears at a window and calls out to them:*
ADÈLE: I'll come and give you a hand! Don't eat all the
    cherries!

In the dining room, the crockery and furniture are being divided into lots, labelled with big numbered stickers: 1, 2, 3. CLAIRE *is standing, playing the piano.* MARIE-LAURE *brings in a pile of plates, smiles at* CLAIRE, *makes a few balletic movements to the music, and goes out again.*

ADÈLE *and* CAMILLE *put a heavy load of silver plate on the dining-room table.*

CLAIRE: No, not in lot number 3! Put it in number 2! It's got far less in it.

(CAMILLE *points to an enormous dresser.*)

CAMILLE: Even with the dresser?

CLAIRE: These big pieces of furniture aren't worth much these days.

CAMILLE: Are you sure?

CLAIRE: You can't fit them into apartments.

CAMILLE: What is the valuable piece, then?

CLAIRE: It's less valuable than I thought.

(MILOU *comes in, Lily's shawl round his shoulders, in high spirits again. He throws the bag of crayfish at* CAMILLE, *who catches it smartly.*)

MILOU: Here, for dinner!

(*He takes a look round.* MARIE-LAURE *reappears, her arms full of books.*)

Well, what a mess we have here! Oh no! You're not sharing out the books!

CLAIRE: Why not?

28

MILOU: Because they're mine! I'm the only one who can read in this family!

(*He goes back into the hallway, where* LILY *and* FRANÇOISE *are standing. He leans towards* LILY.)

I'm going to get changed. I'll be back.

(*He kisses her just above her ear, takes off the Indian shawl and wraps* FRANÇOISE *in it. Then he goes up the stairs, barechested, fist raised, singing the 'Internationale'.* ADÈLE *passes him on the stairs as she comes down, carrying the big dolls dressed in ballgowns.*)

ADÈLE: Where do Aunt Zette's dolls go?

(*Ignoring her,* MILOU *continues up the stairs.*)

MILOU: (*Out of shot*) *L'Internationa–a–a–ale sera le genre humain* . . .

(*From the hallway,* LILY *and* FRANÇOISE *watch him go up the stairs.*)

FRANÇOISE: He's in love!

LILY: Do you know how to make a dry Martini?

FRANÇOISE: A what?

LILY: Come on, I'll show you.

In the library, DANIEL, *the solicitor, is sitting behind a desk, a folder in front of him. The three heirs are sitting opposite, their backs to the body of the dead woman.* MILOU *is in his Sunday best,* CAMILLE *is standing behind him. The room is in a mess, with all the furniture shifted around, divided into lots.*

During the following conversation, LILY *comes in with a cocktail mixer and glasses on a tray, which she puts down on the edge of the desk. She shakes the mixer, and fills the glasses, which* FRANÇOISE *passes round.* LILY *tries to be unobtrusive, but has the opposite result.*

DANIEL *has just finished reading the will. He summarizes:*

DANIEL: Madame Vieuzac has, then, followed the natural order of succession. Her goods are divided between her sons Emile and Georges Vieuzac, and her grand-daughter Claire Dieudonne, the only issue of her deceased daughter Madame Simone Dieudonne, *née* Vieuzac. These goods consist of this property, the land, the furniture and jewellery, and an investment portfolio which is, I believe, pretty negligible.

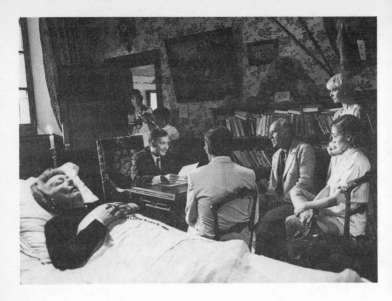

MILOU: Very negligible.

GEORGES: And very neglected.

(*The cat jumps up on to the desk.* DANIEL *pushes it off with his arm.*)

DANIEL: So, it's up to you to decide how you divide things up. I can see that you've already made a start with the furniture. Which leaves the land and the house. You are under no obligation to decide everything today.

GEORGES: We were thinking of selling, but . . .

MILOU: But I don't agree! I don't care if you take the furniture, I'll manage, as long as you just leave me a mattress and my bike!

DANIEL: I must remind you of the rules concerning joint division.

MILOU: What's that?

DANIEL: It means that if the other heirs decide to sell, even just one of them, you can't block it.

MILOU: Well, then let's sell the vineyard!

GEORGES: But what's the vineyard worth? Wine sales are down, we'd have to replant, Léonce is getting old. Who'd be able to look after all that? Certainly not you!

(CAMILLE *comes up to* DANIEL.)

30

CAMILLE: Would you be able to find a buyer for the whole lot?

DANIEL: Could do . . . Yes, probably . . .

GEORGES: Who?

DANIEL: Oh, a group of friends . . . different people . . . It's complicated.

(*The cat jumps up again on to* DANIEL'*s papers, much to his irritation.*)

CLAIRE: And what would they do with it?

DANIEL: Invest, restock the vineyard with different varieties . . . That'd take a lot of money . . . Others say it could be turned into a leisure centre, with tennis, a golf course . . .

MILOU: A golf course? Here?

DANIEL: Yes, this could be the clubhouse, bedrooms in the orangery . . .

CLAIRE: What would we get for it?

DANIEL: Given the state it's in, maybe four hundred thousand francs . . .

MILOU: What?

DANIEL: Four hundred thousand new francs. Forty million old francs.

MILOU: But that's nothing at all! It's hardly the price of the vineyard!

GEORGES: What do you know about it? Prices are tumbling at the moment! Everyone's selling!

MILOU: Well then, we'll wait!

(*They all start talking at once.*)

CAMILLE: But you know very well this house is like a black hole!

CLAIRE: At least we could sell the furniture.

GEORGES: With taxes and running costs, this house can only be run with the family subsidizing it . . . and you're the only one living here!

MILOU: Georges, that's a bit strong!

(DANIEL *gets them to quieten down, with difficulty.*)

DANIEL: Wait, wait a minute! Before you make a decision I have to read you a letter from the deceased.

CLAIRE: A letter?

DANIEL: Yes. She gave it to me about a year ago. (*He shows them the envelope.*) 'To be opened only in the presence of the heirs.' It's usually just some forgotten minor detail . . .

31

CAMILLE: It must be about the ring . . .

(DANIEL *rips open the envelope and begins to read*:)

DANIEL: 'My dear children, I am entrusting this letter to Daniel despite the fact that I have as little confidence in him as in his father.'

(DANIEL *gives a rather forced smile, looks over at the body of Mme Vieuzac, and resumes*:)

'Like the ploughman in the fields, I can feel death approaching, and I must prepare myself for another life in which I fear only one thing: rejoining my husband, without whom I have lived very happily for the last forty-five years. I wish to make only one change to my will, and I'm sure that you will approve, particularly you, Emile. I bequeath a quarter of my worldly goods to Adèle Laborit, the patient friend of these my last years.' It is signed: Elisabeth Marie Vieuzac.

(*Silence.*)

CAMILLE: A quarter of everything?

CLAIRE: Is it legally valid?

DANIEL: Absolutely. She could dispose of a quarter of her goods in whatever way she chose.

GEORGES: A quarter for Adèle! That's a lot!

CAMILLE: Can we contest?

DANIEL: It'd be difficult. Where is Adèle, by the way? I must tell her.

FRANÇOISE: She's picking cherries.

(FRANÇOISE *dashes out of the room.*)

DANIEL: Perhaps Madame Vieuzac had already told her.

MILOU: I doubt it. She didn't like being thanked.

FRANÇOISE *runs out of the house, almost knocking over an elderly lady,* MME ABEL, *wearing a hat and dressed for a visit.*

FRANÇOISE *runs towards the cherry tree in whch* ADÈLE, *basket in hand, is balanced precariously on a branch.*

FRANÇOISE: Adèle! Adèle! You're an heiress!

ADÈLE: What?

FRANÇOISE: You get a quarter of everything!

(ADÈLE *turns round, cries out, loses her balance, and falls. Everyone rushes to pick her up, jostling* MME ABEL. MME ABEL *peers into the drawing room. Behind her,* MILOU,

32

GEORGES, CAMILLE, CLAIRE *and* DANIEL *come into the hallway, carrying* ADÈLE, *who has fainted. They jostle* MME ABEL *again and put the maid down on the sofa. Everyone crowds around.* GEORGES *slaps her gently to bring her round.*)

GEORGES: Come on, Adèle dear, come on . . .

DANIEL: She doesn't look badly hurt.

CAMILLE: (*To* FRANÇOISE) Go and fetch the first-aid kit.

MILOU: I'll get some mustard.

(*He goes out past* MME ABEL.)

MME ABEL: Your poor mother . . .

MILOU: Excuse me. (*Gestures.*) She's in there . . .

(*He steps round her and runs off to the kitchen.* MME ABEL *looks around. She sees the crockery and furniture piled up all over the place. She makes for the library, bumped into this time by* FRANÇOISE *who's on her way back with the first-aid kit.*)

CAMILLE: Will we have to divide things up again?

CLAIRE: Obviously!

(MILOU *returns with the mustard, puts it under* ADÈLE'S *nose.* ADÈLE *gives a start and opens her eyes. Everyone breathes a sigh of relief.*)

ADÈLE: Did I hurt myself?

CAMILLE: No, No. Nothing's broken.

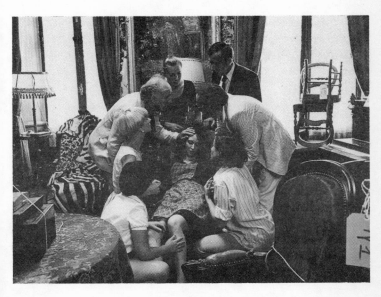

ADÈLE: Naughty girl! You were playing a joke on me!
FRANÇOISE: No! It's true! You're one of the heirs!
CAMILLE: I ought to let Paul know.

In the library, MME ABEL *sprinkles holy water over her friend and starts praying.*
The comings and goings continue around her: the twins chasing each other, CAMILLE *on the way to the telephone,* ADÈLE *being taken into the kitchen . . . Suddenly: shouting, slogans, all the noisy din of a demo in the Latin Quarter fills the room.* MME ABEL *jumps with alarm, and turns round:* GEORGES *is bent over the radio.*
GEORGES: I'm sorry, but it's really hotting up in Paris.
CAMILLE: Hello! Hello! Bordeaux 46.24.30, please! It's urgent! Georges, turn it down!
(LILY *comes back from the kitchen. She's refilled the mixer with dry Martini. She offers a glass to* MME ABEL.)
LILY: (*In English*) Have a drink?
MME ABEL: You're very kind . . .
(MME ABEL *drinks up in one draught, as though it were water. She gives* LILY *a look of astonishment, clutches at her throat, and has a terrible coughing fit.*)
LILY: Too much ice?

A big truck, with 'FRUIT AND VEGETABLES' painted on the side, is driving along the road.
The driver has a moustache, wears a peaked cap, and has a butterfly tattooed on his biceps. Sitting next to him is PIERRE-ALAIN, *Georges's son, twenty-two years old, dark complexion, sharp-featured. He has a plaster on his forehead.*
TRUCK DRIVER: Some *bourgeois* women really fancy all this, you know.
PIERRE-ALAIN: All what?
TRUCK DRIVER: Being on the road, at night, lorries. Can't help themselves. I'm telling you, last month, near Vierzon, there was this really smart woman, black suit, jewellery, gloves up to here. She gets in. Right? Five minutes later, 'May I?' she says, opens my flies, and away we go! She didn't even take her gloves off. Lipstick all over the place afterwards.
PIERRE-ALAIN: Must have been a pro.
TRUCK DRIVER: Not a bit of it. As posh as they come . . . And

34

not the first I've come across. Two years ago, I was driving back from Italy, stopped for a woman and her daughter and as we're going through the Mont-Blanc tunnel all of a sudden – with no prompting from me – the mother says to the daughter, 'Show monsieur . . .'

Dusk. In the Vieuzac's drawing room, the radio is broadcasting de Gaulle's 24 May speech. GEORGES, DANIEL *and* MARIE-LAURE *are gathered around the radio, listening.*
As usual, MARIE-LAURE's *doing her exercises.*
MILOU *sits on the sofa, showing the family album to* LILY, *who's stroking the cat.*
CLAIRE *and* FRANÇOISE *are marking up a set of labels with the number 4.* LÉONCE *comes in, precariously balancing several cases of silver, followed by* ADÈLE *and then* CAMILLE, *who seems beside herself.*

CAMILLE: So what exactly do you want, from the silver? The fish covers? The oyster forks?

ADÈLE: Well, I want a bit of everything.

CAMILLE: We're not going to divide everything four ways. That'd leave us with three forks each! Hardly enough to set a table!

GEORGES: Shush!

(*The women lower their voices. General de Gaulle's voice dominates the scene.* ADÈLE *whispers:*)

ADÈLE: But with what's in the attic as well, you could . . .

CLAIRE: There's more silver in the attic?

ADÈLE: Yes, some incomplete sets. I don't mind if it doesn't match. Just as long as I've got a bit of everything.

CAMILLE: Léonce . . .

(*She gestures upwards. Muttering with annoyance,* LÉONCE *goes off towards the stairs.*)

ADÈLE: I'll go with him, otherwise he won't find it.

(CLAIRE *takes the portrait of a young girl off the wall and examines it.* CAMILLE, *uneasy, comes up to her.*)

CAMILLE: Is this painting worth anything?

CLAIRE: No . . . it's Mother.

(GEORGES *and* DANIEL *are sitting by the radio, discussing de Gaulle's speech.*)

GEORGES: It's bad.

DANIEL: It's not like him at all.

(*On the sofa,* MILOU *shows* LILY *a photograph.*)

MILOU: Here we have Uncle Albert. Mother's uncle. The zebra-skin, up there, was his. He brought it back from Africa.

LILY: The skin, or the zebra?

MILOU: No, the zebra, alive. He'd trained it. He used to harness it up when he had errands to do, and then he'd take it with him when he went to check up on the workers. Once a week, the zebra would bolt and the carriage would overturn.

(LILY *bursts out laughing.* GEORGES *turns round.*)

GEORGES: Shhh!

(LILY *looks at the photo of Uncle Albert.*)

LILY: You look a lot like him.

MILOU: So they say. He was a real character, Uncle Albert! Look.

(*He turns the page and shows her another photo: Uncle Albert in a boat, dressed in hunting gear, a colonial cap on his head, and two young girls, one of whom is in the water, holding a duck.*)

He trained his maids to hunt as well.

LILY: To hunt?

MILOU: Yes, he couldn't stand dogs. Any kind of dog. But he loved hunting. So he'd have the girls in the boat with him and when he'd shot something, they'd jump into the water and swim back with the game!

LILY: No!

(*End of de Gaulle's speech. The 'Marseillaise' plays.* GEORGES *and* DANIEL *seem very disappointed.*)

DANIEL: He's back to his old tricks: the referendum ploy again.

GEORGES: It just won't work. He's completely missed the point, right from the start!

(MARIE-LAURE *leans against* DANIEL *to extend her leg backwards.*)

MARIE-LAURE: He's too old. He really ought to go.

(*The volume of conversation has returned to normal.* CLAIRE'S *voice is heard, calling sharply*:)

CLAIRE: (*Out of shot*) Marie-Laure! Come here!

(*With a rather apprehensive look in her eyes,* MARIE-LAURE *runs over to* CLAIRE, *who takes her to one side.* FRANÇOISE *watches them.*)

What on earth are you doing? I told you to behave!

MARIE-LAURE: I've got every right to say what I think about De Gaulle!

CLAIRE: It's not de Gaulle I'm talking about!

MARIE-LAURE: Then what are you talking about?

CLAIRE: Don't come the innocent with me!

(*She slaps* MARIE-LAURE *across the face.* FRANÇOISE *jumps up,* MILOU *tries to create a diversion.*)

MILOU: Camille! Are you keeping an eye on the crayfish?

CAMILLE: (*From the kitchen*) Nearly ready!

MILOU: Did you put some vinegar in the broth?

CAMILLE: Yes, Father. Don't worry about it.

DANIEL: I'll go and help her.

(*He bounds off to the kitchen.*
Suddenly the electricity cuts out. The sound of a collision and something breaking.)

Oh shit!

GEORGES: Well, that's it. His speech is a flop.

(*Voices in the dark*:)

CAMILLE: Adèle, where are the candles?

37

MILOU: In the kitchen, the drawer to the left of the door.
> (*A beam of light appears, gets nearer to the house and illuminates the drawing room; at the same time a loud engine is heard approaching. Four large headlights come to a halt in front of the ground-floor windows.* LILY *and* MILOU *get up,* FRANÇOISE *comes over and huddles close to them.* CAMILLE *comes back into the room.*)

CAMILLE: What is it now? Father . . . have you got your gun?

MILOU: It's upstairs.
> (*The engine stops, the lights are switched off, doors slam noisily.*
> *Total darkness, except for the candles around Mme Vieuzac. The door opens. Footsteps in the hallway. The flame from a cigarette lighter illuminates a face.*)

A YOUNG MAN: Anybody here?
> (MILOU *bursts out laughing, relieved.*)

MILOU: It's Pierre-Alain. I knew he'd come.
> (PIERRE-ALAIN *takes* GRIMALDI, *the truck driver, by the arm.*)

PIERRE-ALAIN: Come on, come on in.

GRIMALDI: Messieurs–dames . . . (*He sniffs.*) It's dark in here, but something smells good.
> (*He hums a tune: 'Ça sent si bon, la France . . .'*
> ADÈLE *arrives with a candelabra.*
> PIERRE-ALAIN *kisses his father, somewhat coolly.*)

PIERRE-ALAIN: Hello, Father.

GEORGES: Is your mother well?

PIERRE-ALAIN: Fine, asfar as I know. Hello, Milou.

MILOU: What have you done to your forehead?

PIERRE-ALAIN: It's nothing. Just a scratch.
> (CAMILLE, CLAIRE *and* LILY *come over to kiss* PIERRE-ALAIN.)

GRIMALDI: What a sight for sore eyes, such a lovely looking woman. And another one! And yet another one! Well, well!
> (GRIMALDI *has short legs and his movements are light as a dancer's. He's got a Gitane permanently in his mouth, though as often as not it's gone out. When he talks to someone, it's always close up.*)

PIERRE-ALAIN: I'd like to introduce you to Gilbert Grimaldi,

who was kind enough to go out of his way to drop me off.
We're both starving.

CAMILLE: I'll see to it.

(MILOU *draws* PIERRE-ALAIN *towards the library*.)

MILOU: Come and have a look at Mother.

(LILY *comes up to* GRIMALDI.)

LILY: You've come from Paris?

GRIMALDI: Don't ask: the market at Les Halles is closed. I was
bringing in tomatoes from Spain, so I had to turn back.
Then I got stuck in a demo at Denfert. They wanted to set
my lorry on fire, bloody idiots. I managed to get out pretty
quick. Paris is in total chaos, but the approach roads are
completely deserted.

LILY: So you're not on strike, then?

GRIMALDI: Me? That'll be the day. As far as I'm concerned,
the communists can get stuffed.

(*As they talk, they follow the others in to the library. With his
last remark,* GRIMALDI *finds himself face to face with Mme
Vieuzac's body.*)

Oh, excuse me . . .

(*He takes off his cap and stands still, respectfully.*)

Squeezed tight around the candlelit kitchen table, everyone is eating
MILOU's *crayfish. They listen to* PIERRE-ALAIN, *who's holding
forth passionately:*

PIERRE-ALAIN: But that's what's so good! Exactly that! The
fact that they're not demanding anything! Nothing specific.

GEORGES: That's not true of the workers!

PIERRE-ALAIN: But I'm talking about the students, Father!
They were the ones who started it all! And what are they
saying? They're saying: we've had enough of the
profiteering, enough of the rich industrialized countries
deciding everything, enough of bleeding the Earth dry; and
they're saying: Let's stop it now! It doesn't get us
anywhere, it's ridiculous! We're like the rats being led to
the river by the Pied Piper! And we'll drown! There's no
doubt about it! So why don't we stop it all now!

GEORGES: Stop it and do what?

PIERRE-ALAIN: Talk! Think things out and imagine something
else!

CLAIRE: Well, there's no need to build barricades to do that! Or to go round painting slogans on statues!

PIERRE-ALAIN: You're so far away from Paris, the impression you get is exaggerated, distorted. You've just no idea of what's happening, precisely because it's not like anything that's happened before! It's entirely new! People are talking! Just like that! It's totally spontaneous!

GEORGES: Spontaneous, all right, with committees everywhere, offices, cells, Maoists, situationists, those who want this . . .

PIERRE-ALAIN: What's so unusual about people organizing! Or the bourgeoisie resisting! You have to do what's best for people sometimes in spite of themselves. Everyone knows that!

CAMILLE: I've been doing quite nicely up until now, thank you very much! (*She sucks at a crayfish claw with relish, adding, for* PIERRE-ALAIN's *benefit:*) And the pleasures of nature have to be earned.

PIERRE-ALAIN: If you could see Paris right now! Nobody's going to work, there are no more cars, the weather is wonderful, everyone's kissing, people are sharing what they've got, you can feel the joy, the desire, it's like a great party . . .

GRIMALDI: And the rubbish in the streets? Who's going to come and collect it?

PIERRE-ALAIN: It's a minor detail! What matters is that people are coming together, for the first time! Together!

LILY: Are you for de Gaulle, Monsieur Grimaldi?

GRIMALDI: You must be joking! (*He taps his forehead.*) I'm for Grimaldi! Always have been!

PIERRE-ALAIN: You're all blind, just like everybody else! You like to think that everything in this world is just fine, but it's not true! The world is unjust, brutal, disgusting, and it's because of people like you!
(*There's a silence. They stare down into their plates, as though they've been caught out.* MILOU *has dropped food on himself again.*)

MARIE-LAURE: It's true, what he's saying.
(CLAIRE *shrugs her shoulders.*)

GEORGES: Is it true that people are making love all over the place?

PIERRE-ALAIN: Yes – well, those who've got the time.

GEORGES: At the Sorbonne, at Odéon . . .
(GRIMALDI *leans over to* LILY.)

GRIMALDI: At the Sorbonne, apparently, you practically slide over the spunk.

LILY: Ah . . .

FRANÇOISE: Daddy, what's spunk?

CAMILLE: Françoise, go to bed!

FRANÇOISE: I'm not sleepy.
(PIERRE-ALAIN *smiles at her.*)

PIERRE-ALAIN: Yes, at last, people are making love! Just for the pleasure of loving one another. They meet, they like each other, they make love. Foreigners can't get over it!

MILOU: It seems like a dream, what you're saying.

LILY: It makes you feel like going there. It's stupid to miss out on all that . . .

MARIE-LAURE: She's right, it's stupid to stay here, so far away from it all.

PIERRE-ALAIN: Come, then! I'll take you! You can come with me, tomorrow.

MARIE-LAURE: Tomorrow?

PIERRE-ALAIN: I'm going back, after the funeral. I simply must get back. There's bound to be a way! (*To* LILY) You should come as well!

LILY: Well . . .

PIERRE-ALAIN: All of you come!

(*The electricity comes back on, cutting short the general euphoria.* CAMILLE *gets up.*)

CAMILLE: Well, in the meantime, why don't we go to bed? The funeral is at nine . . . Put all the plates back in the piles you took them from, they can be washed tomorrow! (*She blows out the candles, adding:*) Pierre-Alain, I've put you with the kids. (*To* GRIMALDI) I don't know, Monsieur, if you . . .

GRIMALDI: Oh, don't worry about me! I'll sleep in my cabin in the truck! I'm used to it! It's my dream box. (*To* LILY) There's room for two . . .

CAMILLE *goes into the dining room where she finds* ADÈLE, *looking at herself in the mirror, an astrakhan coat round her shoulders.*

CAMILLE: That's Grandmother's coat! But don't let that bother you! Do you know how much an astrakhan is worth?

ADÈLE: Well, since I'm owed so much money already, I said to myself . . . after all . . .

LILY: They're really dreary, those coats.

ADÈLE: I know, but it's warm.

(CAMILLE *takes her by the arm and leads her away.*)

CAMILLE: You'd rather have that than the silver then?

(*Everyone comes over to pile their plates up on the dining-room table.* MILOU *goes up to* LILY.)

MILOU: I don't know if I'll be able to sleep. I've got so much on my mind.

LILY: Me too.

(GEORGES *takes his wife by the shoulder and kisses her neck. He turns to* MILOU.)

GEORGES: Could you lend me a dark suit for tomorrow?

MILOU: Of course I can, Georges.

GEORGES: Good night, Milou.

(LILY *leaves the room, led away by* GEORGES. *She comes*

back to put her plate on the pile. As she does so, she smiles at
MILOU.

MILOU *is left by himself. He looks around at the disordered
room, the numbered labels. He goes through into the hallway
and sees* PIERRE-ALAIN *sitting on the stairs, smoking a
cigarette.*)

PIERRE-ALAIN: Where are you going?

MILOU: To watch over Mother.

(PIERRE-ALAIN *stubs his cigarette out and gets up to go with
him.*

MILOU *stops him at the library doorway.*

ADÈLE *is in there, alone. She's kneeling in prayer, by the side
of the dead woman. Still in the astrakhan coat, she's sweating.*

MILOU *leads* PIERRE-ALAIN *away, sits him down again on
the stairs.*)

Tell me some more . . . about Paris . . .

*Next morning, in front of the house. The sun is still low on the
horizon. It's going to be a glorious day.* GRIMALDI *is shaving
himself at the side of his truck.*

A YOUNG GIRL *on a bicycle pedals briskly into the grounds, ringing
her bell. She stops in front of the entrance to the house and calls out:*

YOUNG GIRL: Monsieur Vieuzac! Monsieur Vieuzac!

(MILOU *appears at a window, in a white shirt.*)

MILOU: What do you want?

YOUNG GIRL: Father told me to tell you that the funeral's off;
it's not possible today.

MILOU: Why not?

(*The* YOUNG GIRL *makes an about turn and goes off.*)

YOUNG GIRL: Because they're on strike! Goodbye!

MILOU: When then? Hey, wait!

YOUNG GIRL: He doesn't know!

*A little later, in the library. They're all gathered around the body,
dressed in mourning, holding cups of milky coffee.*

GRIMALDI *drinks his coffee and suggests:*

GRIMALDI: If you want, you can use the truck to get to the
cemetery.

GEORGES: No. We're not going to send Mother off in a
vegetable truck!

43

CLAIRE: So what are ~~been~~ *(her voice)* She's

Milou - spills coffee again

...oes and while ...ne truck – it's

...ne truck!

MILOU: What if we buried her in the grounds?

CAMILLE: Without a coffin?

MILOU: Surely we can get hold of a coffin. Or make one.

PIERRE-ALAIN: Milou's right.

MILOU: We can put up a memorial to her later on; we could plant a cypress tree. That way we can keep her close by. What do you think, Georges?

GEORGES: It's better than the truck.

CAMILLE: Yes. We can bury her tomorrow morning and then it's all over and done with.

MILOU: I'm going to find Léonce.

(GRIMALDI *stops and stares at* CLAIRE.)

GRIMALDI: You look good in that outfit. Are you wearing stockings or tights?

(CLAIRE *stares at him.*)

At the corner of the barn MILOU, LÉONCE *and* FRANÇOISE *are arguing over where to put the grave.*

FRANÇOISE: Here. It's so pretty . . .

LÉONCE: No! The soil's not deep enough! You'll hit rock almost immediately.

MILOU: What about over there, further down?

LÉONCE: The spring's down there! No, it'd be better to dig next to the big cedar tree.

MILOU: Oh yes, in the shade.

LÉONCE: That'll take me all day, that will.

(*He moves away, grumbling.*)

GEORGES *comes out of the house, carrying the big radio set which he puts on a garden table. He's taken off his jacket and tie and is whistling the 'Internationale'. Through the open window behind him* CLAIRE *can be seen: she's playing the piano. She looks over towards the garden, where* PIERRE-ALAIN, *near to the cherry tree, is taking*

44

off his shirt and showing his back, striped black like a zebra, to
LILY *and* MARIE-LAURE. MARIE-LAURE *shrieks.*

PIERRE-ALAIN: They used a kind of flexible baton, which
  bends to the shape of the body.

MARIE-LAURE: It must be awfully painful!

PIERRE-ALAIN: You get used to it.

LILY: Let me . . .

  (LILY *starts putting cream on the bruises, which* PIERRE-
  ALAIN *identifies, pointing to each one*:)

PIERRE-ALAIN: That one's from the rue Gay-Lussac, that one
  from the Place de la Bourse . . .

  (CLAIRE *continues playing the piano, eyes fixed on* MARIE-
  LAURE. GEORGES *plugs the radio into an extension. He sits
  down in the sunshine and opens his shirt with a satisfied sigh.*)

GEORGES: What a day. In Saint-Tropez, it never stopped
  raining.

LÉONCE *starts digging, at the foot of the big cedar tree.*

FRANÇOISE *and* MILOU *come back towards the house.*

FRANÇOISE *looks at* CLAIRE *at the piano.*

FRANÇOISE: Grandad! Why doesn't Aunt Claire have any
  children?

MILOU: Go and ask her.

FRANÇOISE: I daren't.

MILOU: Me neither.

(*They walk over to* GRIMALDI, *who's unloading crates of tomatoes from the truck.*)

GRIMALDI: Milou, are there any trestle boards around?

MILOU: I think so, over there.

FRANÇOISE: What are you doing?

GRIMALDI: D'you want to help me?

(*Without waiting for an answer, he hands her a boxful.*)
Here, take this and put it down over there, by the tree, along with the others.

(*She moves away, carrying the tomatoes.* GRIMALDI *watches her.*)
She's going to turn out to be a bit of all right. Give her another five or six years, wouldn't mind looking her up again.

(MILOU *gives him a withering look.*)

In the kitchen, CAMILLE *is quietly singing the 'Internationale'. Sleeves pushed back, she's rolling out dough for a quiche, while* ADÈLE *prepared stuffed tomatoes.*

ADÈLE: I wanted to ask you . . .

CAMILLE: Yes, Adèle?

ADÈLE: You know the pills that stop you having babies . . . do you taken them?

CAMILLE: Well, I've been thinking about it, lately . . . but I'm not sure . . .

ADÈLE: What does your husband say? Is it dangerous?

CAMILLE: He says not.

ADÈLE: Then what's stopping you?

(CAMILLE *sees something through the open window.*)

CAMILLE: Hey!

(*She's calling to the twins, who are fighting viciously, kicking and punching.*)
D'you want me to come and sort you out?

(*Outside, the twins continue to chase each other, grabbing each other by the hair, rolling in the grass.* MILOU *goes to separate them.*)

MILOU: Stop it! Just stop it! You know perfectly well neither of
you's going to win! Come on now, enough!
(*In the background,* CAMILLE *reappears at a window in the
dining room.*)
CAMILLE: Go and wash your hands! Father, there's no more
wine!
MILOU: I'll go and get some.
(LILY, *by the cherry tree, gets up.*)
LILY: Wait for me! I'll come with you!
(*She gives the ointment to* MARIE-LAURE *and joins* MILOU,
*taking him by the arm. They go off in the direction of the wine
cellar.*)
MILOU: D'you know the saying by Voltaire? 'I've decided to be
happy because it's good for the health.'

CAMILLE *watches them, from the window, then goes up to* CLAIRE
*who is just finishing, with a flourish, the Debussy prélude she's been
playing in the preceding scenes.*
CAMILLE: Why didn't you go on with the piano?
CLAIRE: Too many pianists . . .
(*She gets up, and goes over to the window.*)
CAMILLE: Shall we go back to dividing things up?
CLAIRE: It's too nice a day.
CAMILLE: Well, if you change your mind.

CLAIRE *watches* MARIE-LAURE *and* PIERRE-ALAIN *under the
cherry tree. He's leaning close to her, talking animatedly:*
PIERRE-ALAIN: I was on the third barricade, at the corner of
the rue St Jacques. About two in the morning, there were
three Bengal lights: the signal for the riot police to attack
with tear-gas. They were throwing chlorine grenades at us,
the bastards . . .
(*At the window,* CAMILLE *turns to* CLAIRE.)
CAMILLE: What's your friend want to do, later on? Become a
dancer?
(CLAIRE *replies, without turning her head, her voice hard:*)
CLAIRE: She'd like to, but she won't make it.

Arms linked, LILY *and* MILOU *make their way down to the wine
cellar.*

LILY: Georges always carries photos of this house around with him. He shows them to everyone.

MILOU: It looks so much grander in photographs. Like me.

LILY: It's true you look alike.

MILOU: The ravages of time . . .

LILY: (*Laughing*) Maybe.

MILOU: I'm even thinking about growing a few vine leaves myself.

(*He gestures with his hands, around his face. She laughs. They go inside the wine cellar, a large room with a high ceiling. The wooden barrels are lined up in rows in the semi-darkness, remnants of a more prosperous past.*)

This used to be the very heart of the house. Let's have a taste of the '65, see how it's getting along. It was the last year we made the wine ourselves.

(*He pours the wine into two glasses.*)

LILY: That smell. It's so sensual . . .

MILOU: I feel that too. The bouquet alone can make you drunk . . .

LILY: We haven't seen each other for so long . . . It's as though I'm getting to know you for the first time . . .

MILOU: To us, then.

(*They link arms to drink from each other's glass, looking into each other's eyes.*)

Do you like it?

LILY: I like it all . . .

In the house, CLAIRE is looking at herself in the big mirror in the hallway. From outside, a radio news bulletin can be heard.

CLAIRE *readjusts herself and goes out. She passes GEORGES, who's bent over the radio, and makes her way over to the cherry tree where MARIE-LAURE and PIERRE-ALAIN are engrossed in discussion.*

PIERRE-ALAIN: But sexual freedom doesn't rule out love – it's just the opposite! It simply rules out the notion of possession. The individual is master of his own body.

MARIE-LAURE: But you can still keep yourself for just one person.

PIERRE-ALAIN: You can, but that's selfishness.

(*He picks a cherry and puts it in MARIE-LAURE's mouth.*

48

MARIE-LAURE *starts when she sees* CLAIRE *sit down next to them.*)

CLAIRE: Am I in the way?

PIERRE-ALAIN: No. Why?

CLAIRE: I usually am.

(*Meanwhile,* GEORGES *listens to the radio:*)

RADIO: While people's action committees are forming everywhere, grievances are being pursued by all kinds of organizations. This morning, the headquarters of the French Football Federation were occupied by a delegation of players led by Just Fontaine. Our reporter, Fernand Choiseul, was there . . .

(*It's a live broadcast: voices punctuate.*)

Football for the players! Football for the players!

(*He reaches out and turns the radio off.*)

GEORGES: Hah! The players!

(*He gets out a handkerchief, folds it into a triangle and puts in on his forehead.*

ADÈLE, *coming back from the wine cellar, stops in front of him.*)

Am I sunburnt?

ADÈLE: Well, I must say, you don't pay much attention to your wife.

GEORGES: Oh you know, after a few months we became an old married couple. But it's not unpleasant.

ADÈLE: She's in the wine-cellar with Milou.

(GEORGES *takes* ADÈLE *by the neck and kisses her.*)

GEORGES: Is Milou nice to you?

(*The solicitor's Alfa-Romeo, roof down, enters the grounds, driving past* LÉONCE, *who's digging, and* GRIMALDI, *who is still unloading his tomatoes, assisted by* FRANÇOISE *and the twins. Some people from the village have gathered round. The Alfa draws up in front of the entrance, where* GEORGES *and* ADÈLE *are standing.* CAMILLE *comes out of the house, carrying a basket.*)

DANIEL: I was waiting for you at the cemetery!

CAMILLE: The undertakers are on strike!

DANIEL: Ah. Where are you off to?

CAMILLE: To look for some eggs.

DANIEL: I'll take you.

(CAMILLE *sits on the bonnet of the car which jolts along towards the barn, circling round the house.* CAMILLE *nearly slides off; laughing, she holds on more tightly.* ADÈLE *follows the car's progress with her eyes.*)

ADÈLE: And where does he manage to get his petrol from?

In front of the barn, DANIEL *executes a sharp turn and brakes suddenly.* CAMILLE *falls off, laughing.* DANIEL *gets out of the car and helps* CAMILLE *up.*
Laughing together, they go into the barn. DANIEL *imitates a cock crowing.*
They stop short, surprised and moved by the silence and beauty of the place.

DANIEL: The orangery! When we used to play in here, it always seemed so enormous. Everything was so cramped at home.

CAMILLE: And I always used to ask: where are the oranges? And they'd reply: Uncle Albert ate them all.
(*A ladder leads to the floor above, where the hay is stored. The sound of chickens clucking.*
They stop at the foot of the ladder, look up, then at each other. CAMILLE *whispers:*)
It was evening on the 14th of July . . . we could hear music . . . we must have been eleven or so . . . You made a formal marriage proposal, do you remember . . .

DANIEL: As if it were yesterday . . .
(*She starts up the ladder. He follows, looking up after her.*)

At the entrance to the grounds, GRIMALDI *has piled up the crates of tomatoes on trestles and, with the help of* FRANÇOISE *and the twins, he's distributing them to the neighbours, among whom we recognize some familiar faces: the* PRIEST, MME ABEL, *the* YOUNG GIRL *from the undertaker's.*

GRIMALDI: Tomatoes, lovely tomatoes! Help yourself! Come on, take advantage! There's a truck full, they're from Andalusia. They have to be eaten before they go off!
(*In exchange, the neighbours offer sausages, cheeses.*)

YOUNG GIRL: My mother told me to give you this. She makes them herself.

GRIMALDI: Thank you, my sweet. Give your mother a nice kiss from me. Come along, come along! Who'd like some lovely tomatoes, free! Lovely love-apples, as they say!

51

MME ABEL: Could I take some for Madame Combes? She's ill
and . . .

GRIMALDI: Why, of course you can! Here, take some for
Madame Combes! And also for Mademoiselle Combes! And
some for all the little Combeses! Come along!

(*Suddenly we hear the 'Internationale', sung very loudly,
interspersed with slogans such as 'De Gaulle at Colombey!',
'We are all German Jews', 'Ten years: enough!'*

LÉONCE *stops his digging for a moment at the sight of about
fifty young people approaching, waving red flags, and even a
black one.*)

What the hell's going on?

PRIEST: They're pupils from the Gambetta secondary school.
Except it's not called Gambetta any more.

GRIMALDI: So what's it called now?

PRIEST: Che Guevara. I was the one who suggested it.

GRIMALDI: I'm not surprised! Well, tell them to come and get
some tomatoes.

PRIEST: They haven't got time. They're too busy making the
revolution.

(*A Citroën enters the grounds, horn blowing to make way
through the demonstrators.*)

FRANÇOISE: It's Dad!
> (*It is, indeed,* PAUL, *dressed in heavy mourning. He gets out of the car.*)

PAUL: Is the funeral over already? What's going on here? Where's your mother?

FRANÇOISE: Well . . .
> (PAUL *shouts out to the company at large:*)

PAUL: Camille . . . Camille!
> (CAMILLE *appears at one of the windows of the barn.*)

CAMILLE: I'm coming.
> (*She disappears back into the barn, where* DANIEL *can be dimly made out, looking around him very cautiously.*
> MILOU *and* LILY *arrive, arms linked, carrying the wine. They're very cheerful.*)

MILOU: The grave-diggers have gone on strike. The funeral's been postponed. So we've decided to put her next to the big cedar tree.

PAUL: You could have let me know! It would have saved me a wasted journey.
> (*He gets back into the car, reverses.* CAMILLE *comes running up, straw in her hair.*)

CAMILLE: Are you going to have lunch with us?

PAUL: Where've you been?

CAMILLE: I was looking for eggs. I'm making quiche.
> (PAUL *glances over to the barn.* DANIEL *comes out, looking nonchalant, bits of straw all over him too.*)

PAUL: I haven't got time for lunch, I've got to be off. You could have phoned me, for Christ's sake! I cancelled at least six appointments so I could come here!
> (*He's already on his way.*)

Picnic on the lawn, underneath the cherry tree. Sheets have been laid out for the food: Camille's quiches, all that the neighbours have brought and, of course, lots of tomatoes. Everyone is stretched out on the grass, and drinking a lot.
LILY lights a joint, which she then passes round. DANIEL is sitting next to CAMILLE, PIERRE-ALAIN next to MARIE-LAURE, LILY between ADÈLE and MILOU, who pulls down a branch of the tree to pick off the cherries.

MILOU: The cherries are delicious this year.

GEORGES: It's so hot!

CLAIRE: Do you think there's going to be a storm?

CAMILLE: It's three days to Whitsun.

MILOU: You're right, I'd forgotten!

FRANÇOISE: We'll be on holiday!

GEORGES: These aren't bad, for Spanish tomatoes.

GRIMALDI: I should hope so . . .

> (CLAIRE *sees* PIERRE-ALAIN *squeeze up against* MARIE-LAURE. *She holds out her glass to* MARIE-LAURE, *who pours for her.* PIERRE-ALAIN *raises his glass.*)

PIERRE-ALAIN: To your health, Aunt.

> (CLAIRE *raises her glass, and drinks it in one go.* LILY *and* ADÈLE *talk to each other in lowered voices.*)

LILY: Well, I always climax really quickly. Too quickly, sometimes. It irritates men. They get the feeling they're redundant.

ADÈLE: It's the opposite for me. It's not that easy for me. What I need is . . .

> (*She whispers into* LILY's *ear. A surprised reaction from the latter.*)

But they never think of that.

LILY: You have to tell them! They can't figure it out all by themselves!

(GRIMALDI *leans over to the two women.*)

GRIMALDI: (*Nostalgically*) The problem with women these days is that they all want an orgasm! Before, they didn't even know it existed. It was a breeze.

(LILY *offers the joint to* MILOU, *who takes it, shooing away the twins, who are sitting on his knees.*)

MILOU: Go and play, kids, go on!

(*He takes a puff, looking deep into* LILY's *eyes.*)

It's my first time. I'll make a wish.

(MARIE-LAURE *is looking amorously at* PIERRE-ALAIN.)

MARIE-LAURE: I'm going to make a wish too.

(PIERRE-ALAIN *pulls her to him and kisses her. The joint now passes to* CLAIRE. *She takes a deep drag and, eyes still fixed on* MARIE-LAURE, *passes it to* GRIMALDI, *who declines, indicating his Gitane.*)

GRIMALDI: No thanks, I smoke French.

(*He gives the joint to* GEORGES, *who passes it without thinking, to* FRANÇOISE. *He asks* GRIMALDI:)

GEORGES: I've gone red, haven't I?

GRIMALDI: No, you haven't.

(GEORGES's *face is as red as a tomato.* FRANÇOISE *passes the joint to her mother and* DANIEL.)

DANIEL: It's really lovely round here.

(CAMILLE *smiles at* FRANÇOISE.)

CAMILLE: It's better than being at the seaside.

DANIEL: If we started from scratch with the vineyards, we could make some truly magnificent wine.

MILOU: Everything's here. Absolutely everything! There's the woods, the vines, fruit, vegetables.

ADÈLE: There's even a spring . . .

(CAMILLE *inhales deeply and chokes.*)

CAMILLE: Yes. And it's even diuretic.

MILOU: Georges, do you remember, once we even thought about exploiting it!

GEORGES: Yes, I remember. But exploit, always 'exploit': to what end?

LILY: You could have a lot of people living here.

PIERRE-ALAIN: Yes! At least a hundred! Maybe even more! We could make a big vegetable garden over there . . .

MILOU: Yes . . .

PIERRE-ALAIN: We could plant apple trees, pears, some corn . . .

MILOU: And there's walnut trees already, that's important. And honey as well.

LILY: I love honey.

CAMILLE: We could increase the poultry stock.

GEORGES: Yes, fresh eggs . . . You should eat an egg a day, that's what Mother always used to say . . . d'you remember . . . ?

CAMILLE: There were goats, too, at one time.

CLAIRE: Oh yes, white goats.

GRIMALDI: It's good, goat's cheese. And it's very stimulating. (*He makes his meaning clear with a gesture.*)

MILOU: And it's easy to make. If we're going to feed more than a hundred people . . .

CAMILLE: We could even sell things . . .

MILOU: I haven't felt this young in thirty years! Long live the Revolution!

PIERRE-ALAIN: Long live the Revolution!

56

(He raises his glass. Everyone follows suit.)
FRANÇOISE: Long live the Revolution!

MILOU, LILY, PIERRE-ALAIN, GEORGES, CLAIRE, FRANÇOISE *and* MARIE-LAURE *walk along in a daydream, carrying their glasses. The twins pick up a flag left behind by the students and wave it in the wind.*

PIERRE-ALAIN: Look, here. It's the ideal spot to install a solar oven. There's bound to be enough sunlight!

MILOU: Surely. And wind, for the windmills. We'll need sheep, for wool.

GEORGES: And rabbits, as well?

LILY: Yes, but then you have to kill them.

MILOU: She's right. We'll eat vegetables.

LILY: The children will be brought up in the midst of nature, they won't go to school any more. It's happening already, you know. In Arizona. And, of course, marriage will have to be abolished.

GEORGES: Of course. To each according to his desires. Women will belong to everyone . . .

(LILY takes MILOU's arm.)

LILY: And the men . . .

MILOU: Marriage is the tomb of love!

CLAIRE: The family destroys children!

MILOU: Oh, to see men and women free! Living in harmony! Sharing everything! I've got to see that before I die . . . (*They pass close by* LÉONCE, *who's still digging the grave, his forehead dripping with sweat.*)

PIERRE-ALAIN: An end to wage slavery. Everyone will choose an occupation that suits him.

GEORGES: Nature's all around. All we have to do is take what she provides. Why should we always want more? So we can die rich? What good will that do us?

MILOU: It's going to spread like wildfire, you know. The whole region will take to it. It's all people are waiting for.

PIERRE-ALAIN: We'll make music, poetry . . . collect vegetable waste to make compost . . .

MILOU: Yes, compost is essential! Egg shells, peelings . . .

GEORGES: We've wasted too much, much too much . . . Just so there can be more plastic, concrete, dead materials . . .

CLAIRE: No more chemicals!

(FRANÇOISE *runs up to* MILOU.)

FRANÇOISE: Grandad! Does it mean we won't have to clean our
     teeth any more?
MILOU: You ask your mother.

They come back to join the others, still stretched out on the lawn.
CAMILLE *is in* DANIEL's *arms. She straightens up when she sees*
FRANÇOISE.
GRIMALDI *half closes his eyes and says:*
GRIMALDI: Ah, this little breeze, the sun, the month of May
     . . . It makes me want to touch a woman's breasts . . .
     (*Suddenly* CLAIRE *kneels down in front of him, opens the
     jacket of her suit, proffers her breasts.*)
CLAIRE: Here . . .
     (*He hesitates for a moment. Everyone looks at him. He cups his
     hands around* CLAIRE's *breasts and caresses them with an
     unexpected delicacy of touch.* CLAIRE *looks at* MARIE-
     LAURE.)
MILOU: Bravo!
     (*They all applaud.*)

Dusk has fallen.
LÉONCE *is still digging the grave.*
MME VIEUZAC *slowly approaches. She's wearing a light summer
dress, and looks a lot younger. She stops at the edge of the grave
and, smiling, watches* LÉONCE *at work. After a moment, he looks
up, looks back at her, expressionless, for an instant, and then returns
to his work.*
The house is in the background, light in the windows.
The sound of the piano.

In the drawing room, CAMILLE *is singing Cherubino's aria from*
The Marriage of Figaro. CLAIRE *accompanies her on the piano.*
CAMILLE: My heart sighs
     Night and day . . .
     (*She faces* DANIEL, *to whom she smiles as she sings.*
     MARIE-LAURE *dances gracefully to the music.* PIERRE-
     ALAIN *can't take his eyes off her. He's on the sofa with*
     FRANÇOISE *and* ADÈLE.)

59

LILY *is sitting on* MILOU'*s knee. He's engrossed in her cleavage.*
GRIMALDI *turns the pages of the score for* CLAIRE.
CAMILLE *sings rather awkwardly, but with great feeling. Suddenly* GEORGES, *his face hidden behind a large African mask, and with a straw skirt round his waist, bursts into the room, singing at the top of his voice the Bedouin Daughter's aria, from the operetta* Le Comte Obligado, *a catchy pasodoble.*)

GEORGES: The bedouin's daughter
        followed this caravan
        night and day . . .
        She was dying of love
        for a young bedouin
        in the ca–ra–van . . .

(*Immediately, the atmosphere changes.* CLAIRE *starts to accompany him on the piano,* MARIE-LAURE *and* FRANÇOISE *dance with him. The others beat out the rhythm with their hands, or on nearby objects.*
MILOU *and* LILY *get up to join the dance.* GEORGES *waddles along to the beat, in an improbable imitation of a camel.*)
    And the little donkey man

In the banana tree
nicking the bananas
which the bedouin's daughter
was carefully putting away
in her little basket! . . .

(GRIMALDI *takes a napkin and makes a chador with it. He
leads everyone in an African conga dance. They go through the
dining room, past the foot of the stairs, where the twins, who
have got out of bed, are looking on in dismay. The dance
continues into the library, around Mme Vieuzac's body, much
to the fury of the cat.*
At the music's finale, GEORGES *takes off his mask.*
Enthusiastic applause. MILOU *takes the mask and shows it to*
CAMILLE.)

MILOU: Do you remember, it belonged to Uncle Albert? One
day he put it on to go to Mass!

GEORGES: And took his zebra!

CAMILLE: Oh yes, and the two maids as well. Héloïse and . . .
what was the other one called?

MILOU: Maryvonne.

CAMILLE: He used to say, 'I'm taking my harem to Mass.'

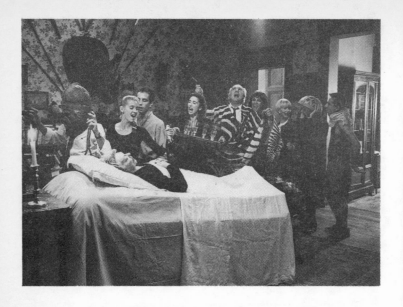

GEORGES: And he used to knock at their door, saying, 'Nature calls!'

MILOU: He was a man ahead of his time!

GEORGES: Ah, what a shame he couldn't be here now!

CAMILLE: He'd be taking his zebra to the Sorbonne!

(GEORGES, *still with the straw skirt round his waist, holds out his empty glass to* ADÈLE. *Getting his breath back he says, in a very serious tone of voice:*)

GEORGES: In fact, what all the great social reformers were missing was the Pill. If you take genetic necessity away from sex what you get is pleasure. Pure pleasure! With no second thoughts! In a word – happiness!

MILOU: We must learn not to be ashamed of physical love.

GEORGES: That's right! What could be more beautiful than two naked bodies giving pleasure to one another?

MILOU: We have to learn to make love in front of other people! It would change everything!

(CLAIRE *nods vigorously in agreement. She drinks her glass in a single draught, throws it behind her and plants herself in front of* MILOU.)

CLAIRE: Yes! Yes! A very good idea! And we can start right

now! So: we'll all write our names on pieces of paper, men
here, women there, and we draw lots for each couple. OK?

CAMILLE: And then?

CLAIRE: And then they'll make love right here and now . . .

CAMILLE: In front of Grandmother?

CLAIRE: By now, Grandmother must be . . .
(*She folds the paper with her name on it and puts it into a jar.*)
There! I'm ready!
(*They all look at her – especially* MARIE-LAURE – *with some
surprise.* GRIMALDI *goes over to her.*)

GRIMALDI: I'm willing!
(ADÈLE *makes a step towards the door.*)

ADÈLE: I've got to get home, Mother is all by herself. . .
(MILOU *grabs her by the hand, holding her back.*)

MILOU: No, no, you stay here. You can't leave now!

CLAIRE: So? Nobody else?
(CLAIRE *turns to* GRIMALDI.)
Well, then, Monsieur Grimaldi, since we're the only ones,
we can start whenever you're ready . . .
(GRIMALDI *hesitates a moment.*)

GRIMALDI: Please . . . after you.

CLAIRE: Very well!
(*She takes off her jacket, hands it to* GEORGES, *then stands
facing* GRIMALDI.)
Will you give me a hand?

GRIMALDI: Right away.
(*He begins to unbutton the numerous buttons on her blouse,
taking his time.*
Everyone watches, ADÈLE *with her eyes popping out,* LILY
leaning against MILOU . . . CAMILLE *fusses over*
FRANÇOISE, *unconvincingly:*)

CAMILLE: Go to bed.

FRANÇOISE: No!
(*She sees* DANIEL, *aroused, put his arm round* CAMILLE's
waist.
MILOU *gathers* FRANÇOISE *up in his arms. He's radiant. He
murmurs to her:*)

MILOU: I think the house is saved.
(CLAIRE *shrugs the blouse off her shoulder. It falls to the floor,
revealing her breasts.*

63

GRIMALDI *picks up the blouse. It's clear he doesn't know what to do with himself.*)

CLAIRE: You're getting a hard-on, Monsieur Grimaldi?

GRIMALDI: It's coming along.

(Suddenly there's a very loud knock on the door, followed by several more.

Everyone freezes, looking at each other.

CAMILLE *goes to open it.*

She opens the front door. As if from nowhere: a MAN *and a* WOMAN *we haven't seen before, loaded with bags and parcels. They're dressed in rather elegant hunting gear. He has a gun, she a rifle. She's also carrying a little dog in her arms.)*

CAMILLE: Ah . . . So it was you? Good evening . . .

WOMAN: May we come in?

CAMILLE: Yes, of course, do come in. What's the matter?

(The newcomers go into the drawing room.)

MILOU: Monsieur Boutelleau! Madame Boutelleau! What's happened?

BOUTELLEAU: You haven't heard?

(GEORGES, still wearing his straw skirt, comes up and asks:)

GEORGES: Heard about what?

BOUTELLEAU: It's started!

64

GEORGES: What? What's happened?

BOUTELLEAU: It's started! Tonight's the night! They've occupied the factory and locked up my foremen! We thought we'd better leave the house.

(CLAIRE *comes up.*)

CLAIRE: Really?

MME BOUTELLEAU: Well, after the threats we've received! . . . (*She shoots a surprised glance at* CLAIRE. *The latter suddenly remembers that she's half naked. She crosses her arms over her breasts, and hurriedly looks for her blouse.*

GEORGES: It might not be all that serious, you know . . .

MILOU: They want to talk . . . it's in the air.

BOUTELLEAU: Didn't you hear the news? De Gaulle has left Paris!

EVERYONE: What?!

BOUTELLEAU: Nobody knows where he is, he might be dead. And that German anarchist is back. Cohn-Bendit!

MME BOUTELLEAU: He gave a press conference in Paris!

EVERYONE: No!

BOUTELLEAU: There are red flags everywhere. Dozens of trucks have been seen leaving Montauban and Agen. It's all been organized. And they're armed! No, I tell you, it's all over now! Pompidou's going to resign, if he hasn't already.

MME BOUTELLEAU: He might be in Switzerland by now.

BOUTELLEAU: The communists have decided to blow things apart. It's obvious! So there's a power vacuum! An absolute vacuum! Everything's falling apart.

DANIEL: What about the army!

BOUTELLEAU: The army's divided amongst itself! We can't count on the army!

MME BOUTELLEAU: And you know, the Russian tanks are two days away from Strasburg.

(GEORGES *has rushed over to the radio. He turns the knobs, the signature tune of Europe 1:*)

RADIO: The latest headlines . . . Jacques Paoli . . . Good evening. We've just heard: Monsieur Georges Pompidou . . .

(*Just at this moment, the electricity goes off again.*)

GEORGES: Not again!

(*In the darkness, sounds and cries.*)

MME BOUTELLEAU: It's the signal, the whole of France is in darkness now.

GRIMALDI: Don't move! I'll put the headlights on!
(*He makes a rapid exit. Silence.*)

MILOU: Have you eaten, at least?

MME BOUTELLEAU: No, but I had a good leg of lamb, I brought it along. It'd be a shame to waste it.
(*The headlights suddenly illuminate the drawing room.* CAMILLE *takes the situation in hand.*)

GEORGES: Milou, what are we going to do?

CAMILLE: Listen to me! We can't stay here, it's too dangerous!

MILOU: Why?

CAMILLE: Why? Because we'd be first in the firing line, that's why! Because of the house.

MME BOUTELLEAU: She's right. They're quite capable of burning it down!
(GRIMALDI *comes back into the room.*)

GRIMALDI: There's going to be rape everywhere, I'm telling you.

CAMILLE: Françoise, go and wake your brothers, we have to leave!

LILY: Leave? But where shall we go?

PIERRE-ALAIN: They can't do anything to me. I'm on their side.

BOUTELLEAU: That's what you think! As far as they're concerned, you're your father's son, and that's all there is to it!

DANIEL: We're all in the firing line! And me first of all!

MILOU: But . . . but me . . . I've never harmed a soul!

CAMILLE: You own property, Father! You're a capitalist!

MILOU: Me?

CAMILLE: Yes, you!
(BOUTELLEAU, *lectures* PIERRE-ALAIN.)

BOUTELLEAU: Don't kid yourself. We're not in the Latin Quarter now! They'll have you up against the wall quick as a shot! In these situations there's no room for argument. Just remember the Spanish Civil War. Shoot first, ask questions later! Just like here in 1944!

MME BOUTELLEAU: Even now there might be thousands dead.
(*They are all silent, wild-eyed, indecisive. Just at that moment*

two fighter planes fly over the house, at very low altitude, making an almighty noise. GEORGES *grabs* MILOU's *arm.*)

First light of day, just before dawn. They are all setting out for the mountain: the BOUTELLEAU *couple,* DANIEL, CAMILLE, GEORGES, LILY, MILOU, FRANÇOISE, *the twins, all heavily laden down – the donkey as well – carrying bags, tools.* PIERRE-ALAIN *and* MARIE-LAURE *are side by side, slightly apart from the others.* CLAIRE *is last. With her weak ankle, she's losing ground.* GRIMALDI *helps her.*

Climbing with difficulty, they reach the edge of the forest. CLAIRE *is now sitting on the donkey's back.* MILOU, *who's carrying a rifle on his shoulder, turns round to ask* CAMILLE:

MILOU: You didn't forget the salt?

CAMILLE: No . . . I brought some aspirin, as well. Don't worry.

    (GEORGES *asks* LILY *anxiously:*)

GEORGES: Did you bring my laxative?

LILY: Oh no . . .

GEORGES: Oh.

    (*They plunge into the trees.*)

The sun's shining, it's hot. They are sitting in a clearing, heartily eating Mme Boutelleau's leg of lamb. MILOU *cuts himself a decent slice.* MME BOUTELLEAU *gives him a black look.*

MME BOUTELLEAU: A good leg of lamb will do for seven or eight, but no more than that.

CAMILLE: Would you like some ham?

DANIEL: The trouble with ham is that it makes you thirsty.

(GEORGES *is whittling away meticulously at a piece of wood.*)

FRANÇOISE: What are you making?

GEORGES: A whistle. We'll have to organize a rota for sentry duty, hmm?

(*He puts the whistle to his lips and blows: to no effect.*)

Right! I'm off to set traps.

(*He moves away.*)

MILOU: (*To* LILY) He made a fine Boy Scout, you know!

(GEORGES *passes the twins, who are crouched behind a bush, pants down, looking tragic.*)

GEORGES: You've got the runs? You're lucky!

(GEORGES *is trying to set up a trap, with a large stone balanced against a small twig. He explains to* FRANÇOISE, *who watches him:*)

It needs to be very finely balanced . . . You put some seeds underneath, there . . . the bird approaches . . .

(*Demonstrating his words with the appropriate gesture,* GEORGES *puts down some seeds that he's brought with him.*)

. . . and when he brushes against the twig . . .

(*He moves clumsily and the heavy stone falls on his fingers. He jumps up with a cry of pain.*

FRANÇOISE *points out something down below. What he sees makes him very anxious.*)

FRANÇOISE: Uncle Georges! Look!

(*In the distance, he sees a group of men on the way up. They look as though they're carrying arms, and what might be a mortar gun in a casing.*

GEORGES, *very worried, leads* FRANÇOISE *away.*

They come running back to the others, out of breath.)

GEORGES: Quickly! There's a whole group coming up! They're armed! We can't stay here! Come on! Get moving!

(*Everyone gets up, frantic.* GEORGES *urges them on.*)

Quickly! This way! Leave everything here!

*(Abandoning their equipment and provisions, even the donkey,
they rush off into the thickets.*
CAMILLE *comes back frantically for the twins.*
*Shortly afterwards five or six men come into view. They are
obviously woodcutters. What looked like a mortar gun is a
chainsaw in a casing.*
*They seem surprised to find the fire and the remains of the meal.
One of them takes a piece of ham and eats it. They gather
round the donkey, talking animatedly in local dialect.)*

The others are scrambling up a slope in the thicket.
DANIEL *has cut his hand and it's bleeding. The twins are crying.*
GRIMALDI *is helping* CLAIRE.
*Suddenly, the sound of a chainsaw. They stop for a moment,
listening hard.*
GRIMALDI: It couldn't be woodcutters?
GEORGES: We were right to be careful though.
    (They continue to climb with difficulty.)

*Night has fallen. In the distance, thunder rumbles. They sit,
exhausted, around a big fire. They cover themselves as best they can
under two blankets. They watch the menacing shadows which
surround them. The twins huddle close to their mother, whimpering.*
GEORGES: What'll be the legacy of the de Gaulle era, when all's
    said and done? Not much.
MILOU: Well, they'll say he bungled his exit.
GEORGES: He didn't see any of it coming. Not a thing . . .
    strange, all the same.
LILY: He was a military man.
    (GRIMALDI has put his jacket round CLAIRE's shoulders.)
GRIMALDI: Are you cold?
CLAIRE: No, hungry.
GRIMALDI: When I think of all my lovely tomatoes . . .
MME BOUTELLEAU: My grandfather was an officer in the Navy.
    Once he had to eat a man's thigh . . .
GRIMALDI: Really?
MME BOUTELLEAU: They were lost at sea, with no food, so
    they took one of the wounded and then . . . !
BOUTELLEAU: It's hardly the time to tell stories like that!
GRIMALDI: And did he like it?

MME BOUTELLEAU: No . . . but then he had to eat it raw.
   (*Everyone's looking at them. A long pause . . .*)
CAMILLE: What if we went back to fetch the supplies?
MILOU: In the middle of the night?
   (*He gets up to put a log on the fire.* GEORGES *takes him aside.*)
GEORGES: Milou . . . Don't say anything to Lily, but I've been
   fired from the paper.
MILOU: Really?
GEORGES: They're going to replace me, in London . . . with a
   younger man.
MILOU: Is that why you wanted to sell the house?
GEORGES: Don't worry, I'll be all right . . . there's my book
   . . . if they still publish books.
   (*They come back towards the others.*)
FRANÇOISE: Grandad?
MILOU: What?
FRANÇOISE: Do revolutions go on for a long time?
MILOU: Depends.
CLAIRE: And what about you, Pierre-Alain, what have you got
   to say about all this?
PIERRE-ALAIN: I'm tired.
   (BOUTELLEAU *looks at* PIERRE-ALAIN.)

BOUTELLEAU: I'm going to tell you something: I hate young people.

(*Just at this moment the first drops of rain begin to fall.*)

MME BOUTELLEAU: Rain . . . That's all we need!

CAMILLE: And we didn't bring umbrellas!

(*Everyone wakes up, tries to find shelter. It's now a heavy downpour.*)

GEORGES: Hey, Milou, isn't there a grotto somewhere round here?

MILOU: Yes, there is . . . Higher up . . . It was used as a hide-out by the Resistance during the war.

GEORGES: Let's go! We'll follow Milou! Everyone hold hands!

(*In the darkness, they stumble on the sodden ground, fall down, get up, grabbing on to thorny branches, and try to follow* MILOU *through the wood.* GRIMALDI *carries* CLAIRE *on his back.*)

MILOU: I think it's over there, but I'm not exactly sure . . .

CAMILLE: Ow!!!

(DANIEL, *emerging from a thicket, unwittingly lets a branch snap back into* CAMILLE's *face.*)

You could be more careful! I'm right behind you!

DANIEL: Well, watch where you're going!

Camille - annoyed - whacked by a branch.

(GEORGES *falls into a ditch*.)

GEORGES: Argh! Oh shit! Milou, help me!

MILOU: I'm here, I'm here.

(MILOU *and* LILY *help him out of the ditch.* GEORGES *is covered with mud.*

CAMILLE, *furious, turns on* PIERRE-ALAIN.)

CAMILLE: See where it gets us, your stupidity!

GEORGES: It's easy to stir it up! It's easy to tear up the pavements shouting 'You're all a bunch of idiots!'

PIERRE-ALAIN: But this isn't what we wanted! It's other people taking advantage of us!

CAMILLE: You should have thought of that before! Now, the children are sick, we're starving to death, the house might be burned down!

CLAIRE: And your husband might be dead.

GEORGES: 'O brave new world!' You must be joking! As if the world was waiting for you lot . . . !

GRIMALDI: It's easier to get the toothpaste out of the tube than to get it back in.

PIERRE-ALAIN: You're talking rubbish! You don't understand anything! You're hopeless, the lot of you! You're too old!

(GEORGES *lunges at* PIERRE-ALAIN, *hitting him hard*.)

GEORGES: That's enough. Just shut up!

(PIERRE-ALAIN *is about to hurl himself at his father, but* GRIMALDI *holds him back.*)

PIERRE-ALAIN: You don't even hit as hard as the cops!

(MILOU *backtracks*.)

MILOU: I think it's lower down. We need to go right.

(*They move off.*

The BOUTELLEAUs *who've kept to the rear, follow.*

MME BOUTELLEAU *takes something from her pocket and gives it surreptitiously to her husband and to her dog.*)

MME BOUTELLEAU: Bernard! . . . Here . . . some chocolate.

They're now in a grotto, covered with mud, wet through, scratched all over. They huddle around a fire which gives off a lot of smoke, making them all cough. GEORGES *fiddles desperately with the Boutelleaus' small transistor radio.*

BOUTELLEAU: Don't get yourself worked up. The batteries are dead.

(GEORGES *flings the radio away.*)

GEORGES: It's awful, not knowing what's going on . . .

LILY: Would you like me to go down and see if I can find *Le Monde?*

(GEORGES *gives her a black look.*)

GEORGES: Stop giving me a hard time.

(CAMILLE *opens her bag to look for a handkerchief.* CLAIRE *notices Mme Vieuzac's jewellery box.*)

CLAIRE: You brought the jewellery? All of it?

CAMILLE: Of course I did! I wasn't going to leave it there!

MME BOUTELLEAU: I brought mine as well.

CLAIRE: And do you intend to keep it?

CAMILLE: Why do you ask?

CLAIRE: Because at times I get the feeling you want to hold on to everything! The furniture, the jewels, the silver! The jewels are always excluded from the division of goods. Jewellery always goes to the daughters!

MME BOUTELLEAU: That's quite true.

CLAIRE: And my mother was the only daughter.

CAMILLE: And my daughter is the only grand-daughter.

CLAIRE: You'd already taken the emerald before I got here, and now you want to swipe all the rest!

73

CAMILLE: Go on, call me a thief!

CLAIRE: You're not the heir! I've already told you! It's your father who inherits, not you!

CAMILLE: Granny wanted the emerald to go to Françoise! That's why she gave it to me! I've got three children, you know! I've got to think of them! You won't have anybody to worry about after you're gone! Dykes don't have kids! Anyway, take them, go on, here, since you want them so much!

(*She throws the box at her. The jewels fall all over the ground.* CLAIRE *grabs* CAMILLE. *They fight, using fists and handbags.* MARIE-LAURE *tries to restrain* CLAIRE, *who shoves her away angrily.*)

CLAIRE: Leave me alone, you!

DANIEL: Camille, stop it!

(*Those trying to separate the two women get drawn into the fray.* GRIMALDI *grabs* CLAIRE *by the hips.*)

CLAIRE: Get your hands off me, truck driver!

(*Suddenly* CAMILLE *breaks down. She weeps in* DANIEL's *arms.*)

CAMILLE: She hates me! Everyone hates me! . . . I look after everyone, take care of everything, work from morning till night, do all the cooking, and everyone just takes advantage of me!

DANIEL: Oh, come on now . . .

CAMILLE: You more than anyone! You're a bastard! A real bastard! You're only looking for kicks. You don't know the first thing about women!

(MILOU *and* FRANÇOISE *have stayed quietly by the fire.*)

FRANÇOISE: Grandad?

MILOU: Yes?

FRANÇOISE: What's a dyke?

(*For once,* MILOU *replies harshly to her.*)

MILOU: I don't know!

(*As if to make amends, he takes her by the shoulder and holds her close.*)

Early morning in the forest. MILOU *is perched on an overhanging rock looking out over the valley. He hears a sound behind him. It's* LILY.

MILOU: You can see houses down there.

(*She climbs up beside him. In the distance, a cluster of houses in a small hamlet can be dimly made out.*)

I always wake up very early. I love watching the day break.

LILY: Often, I'm just going to bed.

MILOU: They say that looking at beautiful landscapes gives you beautiful eyes . . .

(*They stay silent for a moment. LILY shivers.*

MILOU *takes off his jacket and puts it round LILY's shoulders.*)

LILY: You'll catch cold . . .

MILOU: So what if I catch cold?

(*She squeezes up a little closer to him. Another brief pause. They listen to the birds singing.*)

LILY: What are you thinking about?

MILOU: I'm thinking of Mother, all alone down there . . . About you, and me and the house . . . about all those things . . . Can you smell the honeysuckle?

(MILOU *and* LILY *are making their way back to the grotto.* GEORGES *appears, clutching his back. They hear someone calling.* ADÈLE *appears, pulled along by Léonce's dog. She's carrying a basket of food.*)

Adéle!

ADÈLE: There you are! I was so worried! It was Léonce's dog who tracked you down, even with all the rain. I think you can go back down now.

GEORGES: What's happening?

ADÈLE: De Gaulle came back, he made a speech. There was a big parade on the Champs-Elysées last night, but for him this time, an enormous crowd, it seems, and this morning everything's back to normal!

(*One by one, the others emerge from the grotto, haggard and unshaven. They listen to* ADÈLE *who shouts:*)

It looks like it's all over! There's going to be an election! And you can get petrol, everywhere! François Mauriac was at the parade . . .

They reach the house, tired and dirty. They look ░ *f they'd been in*
the woods for weeks. The sound of car horns.
Two undertakers are putting mourning hangings o░░ ░ntrance
door.

In the library a young man in policeman's uniform ░░ ░ng near
Mme Vieuzac's body, twirling his cap in front of h ░
He gets up when he sees CAMILLE *arrive. She look* ░
astonished. GEORGES, MILOU, CLAIRE *and* ADÈ░ ░ *in after*
her, the latter taking the young man's arm.
ADÈLE: I'd like to introduce you to Marc, my fian░ ░e're
    getting married this summer . . .
    (*The* POLICEMAN *bows.*)
MARC: Pleased to meet you . . .
    (*Silence. They all look at him.* GEORGES *shakes* ░░░░ ░he
    others follow suit.)

The whole family is lined up outside the cemetery to shake hands.
GRIMALDI, LÉONCE *and* DANIEL *file by, along with* ADÈLE *and*
MARC. ADÈLE *kisses* GEORGES, MILOU, CAMILLE, CLAIRE.
She's wearing the astrakhan coat. She's hot and wipes her forehead
with a small handkerchief. PAUL, CAMILLE's *husband, is there.*

MILOU *looks at* MARC, CAMILLE *and* DANIEL *avoid each other's eyes.* CLAIRE *shakes* MARIE-LAURE's *hand.*

They leave the cemetery.
PIERRE-ALAIN *and* MARIE-LAURE *walk rapidly towards her 2CV. A wave to the others, and they're off.*
CLAIRE *watches them go without moving a muscle.*
GRIMALDI *climbs into his truck, turns round.* CLAIRE *makes a sign with her hand, smiles.*

CLAIRE *and* GEORGES *are in the library, sitting in front of the desk.* DANIEL, *bent over, hands them a document.*
DANIEL: You initial here, and here; you sign there.
   (*They sign, watched by* MILOU *who's standing, arms folded, in the hallway.*)

The family disperses in front of the house. GEORGES, LILY *and* CLAIRE *get into the Rover.* LILY *and* MILOU *exchange a last glance.*
CAMILLE *and* PAUL *pile parcels into the Citroën.*
Down at the bottom of the grounds, LÉONCE *is filling in the grave.*
MILOU *walks slowly towards the trees.* FRANÇOISE *catches up with him and takes his hand.*

They reach the river, the spot where MILOU *went fishing for crayfish. Suddenly he runs up to the riverbank.*

MILOU: Oh, the bastard!

> (*The surface of the water is covered with dead fish, floating belly up. On the opposite riverbank a man on horseback rides by at a trot, reining in his horse. It's* BOUTELLEAU. *He looks triumphant.*
>
> MILOU *explodes with rage. He runs along the riverbank, shaking his fist at* BOUTELLEAU.)
>
> Murderer! Polluter! Shithead! Disgusting! Garbage! Pimp! Exploiter! Industrialist! Hypocrite! Mercenary!

FRANÇOISE: What's the matter, Grandad?

MILOU: It's that bastard Boutelleau! He took advantage of the situation to drain his vats. It'll all be blamed on the strike.

> (*The sound of a car horn and* CAMILLE'*s voice: 'Françoise!'*)

FRANÇOISE: They're waiting for me.

> (*The two of them embrace.*
>
> MILOU *is alone.*
>
> *He comes back towards the house. The shutters are closed.*
>
> *He goes in.*
>
> *The hallway, the dining room: completely empty, not a stick of*

*furniture nor a picture is left. Just Milou's bike, leaning against
the wall.*
MILOU *hears piano music, like a music box. He goes into the
drawing room, where the furniture is grouped into lots in a
corner.* MME VIEUZAC *is sitting at the piano, near the
window. She smiles at* MILOU. *She's playing, now,* Allegro
vivace.
*She gets up, and the music continues.
She dances with her son.)*